Vengeance at Blackstone

Self-exiled from his home-town for two years after he killed a man in a shoot-out, Benjamin Cage now plans to return to Blackstone, Texas. On the way, he fights and finally captures a ruthless and perverted murderer. Reaching Blackstone, Cage finds the town terrorized by a mining company's hired gun. When the gunman murders the town's marshal Cage must face uneven odds to confront the killer.

Meanwhile, he learns that the murderer he captured has escaped and plans to take vengeance on him by kidnapping his lover and torturing her to death.

His plans for a trap confounded by a daring bank robbery, Ben must summon all his courage and skills to face a bizarre and horrifying final battle.

Vengeance at Blackstone

Wade VanMarten

A Black Horse Western

ROBERT HALE · LONDON

© Wade VanMarten 2004
First published in Great Britain 2004

ISBN 0 7090 7634 7

Robert Hale Limited
Clerkenwell House
Clerkenwell Green
London EC1R 0HT

Typeset by
Derek Doyle & Associates, Liverpool.
Printed and bound in Great Britain by
Antony Rowe Limited, Wiltshire

CHAPTER 1

Benjamin Cage usually slept deeply and very well. This night was an exception and he lay in the bed listening to Karalou breathe softly. They had made love three times before drifting off to sleep. She had been loath to sleep, clinging to him tightly even after they had sated their needs for one another. He supposed it was her way of hanging on as long as possible because she knew he would leave at dawn. He had been unable to promise that he would be back despite the way he felt about her, and his conscience was the demon disturbing his night's sleep. Her affection for him had led her to give herself to him completely, without reservation or conditions, even knowing that he would probably ride away sometime in the future. Now that future had arrived.

He and Johnny Chance had taken jobs with Wiley Golightly for a drive of 2000 head of beef to Dodge City. They had lingered in Fort Worth long enough and they were running out of money. Johnny's usual success at the poker-table had eluded him lately and his reserves were running low.

But even more pressing than that was the pull that Cage felt for his home, Blackstone, in north Texas. It had been two years since he had ridden out, hounded like a pariah because of Harvey Oleman's death. Oleman was a thief and Cage knew it. But when Cage challenged him, Harvey tried to kill him. To save his own life, Cage had shot Oleman in a public place, in front of witnesses. It was a fair fight and no criminal charges were filed. But his explanations for the confrontation fell on deaf ears. Oleman was loved by many and he handled money for many people who expected to get rich. When Cage rode out of town, he intended never to return. In his mind's eye, he could see Sophie on the boardwalk in front of the general store, weeping uncontrollably as she watched him ride out.

Now, though, he was thinking of returning.

Through Karalou's window, he saw that the eastern sky had lightened. He and Johnny had to get an early start to make it to Golightly's spread by suppertime. He got up and dressed quietly. After he pulled on his boots, he noticed that Karalou's breathing had changed. He glanced at the bed. She was lying on her side facing him, watching him dress. He got up and leaned over and kissed her, tasting her salty tears.

*

Benjamin Cage stood an inch over six feet. He was broad-shouldered and muscular, with a face that looked hewed out of stone, a face that other men might regard as handsome and women would look upon as disquieting. In contrast with his black hair, his eyes were dark blue, deep-set and piercing, but subtly softened by a hint of sadness.

Johnny Chance was shorter by two inches, sandy-haired, brown-eyed and stolid of build. He was almost baby-faced and his demeanor as rarely serious. His natural, unaffected boyishness along with his innocent face and sense of humor provoked the maternal sense in females, an instinct of which he took full advantage.

The pair of riders arrived at the Golightly spread just in time to tow their gear and attend the new hires' meeting with Golightly and his trail boss. Golightly met with them outside the bunkhouse and told them that he had a contract to deliver 2000 head to Dodge City by the end of September and that the pay was thirty-five dollars a month.

He added: 'The drive is a fairly short one; you'll make only a month's pay for it. For that reason and the fact that this is probably the last long drive I'll be involved in, I'm going to add a fifteen-dollar bonus to each man's pay if you get the herd to Dodge on time and with a full count.'

The men looked at one another, smiling and nodding. Then one of them asked:

'Did you say this is your last drive?'

'You heard correctly, son,' Golightly answered. 'The homesteaders are moving in and stringing wire and making the trail-drive job a hell of a lot harder. The railroad is getting to be a better way to move stock and it's faster. The times have changed, and we have to change with them or lose out.'

The men grew silent and Golightly continued: 'But back to the drive; I think you will find that the chuck will be as good or better than you can get on any drive in this part of the world. Mobley, your trail cook, is one of the best in the business. Now that that's said, this is Matt Stevenson over here. He's your trail boss and what he says goes.'

Matt Stevenson stood a broad-shouldered five foot ten and looked as strong as an ox. His sleeves were rolled up to above the elbow, revealing thick sinewy arms. He had a square jaw, deep-set brown eyes and a weathered face set off by a fierce mustache. He wore a Walker .44 on his right hip. He spoke in a strong voice.

'Tomorrow morning, first thing, each of you look at the remuda and pick out ten horses to use on the drive. Paul Booher is the horse-wrangler. Let him know which ones you've picked out for yourself and he'll mark them. The others will be left here. After that, there's a few dozen head of beef that need trail brands. We'll get that done tomorrow afternoon. We move out day after tomorrow at dawn. After I've had a chance to size you up, I'll name my *segundo*. In case any of you were wondering, there'll be no drinking on the trail except when you have leave to visit some of those towns along the way. You can tie on the bear in the saloons and whorehouses but stay sober on the job. Any questions?'

There were none.

'All right,' Golightly announced. 'Mobley has got some chuck cooked up for you. Take off and get your supper and pick out a vacant space in the bunkhouse if you haven't already. Enjoy it as this is the last time you'll be sleeping on anything as luxurious as a cot for at least a month.'

Cage and Johnny joined the others as Mobley dished out fried chicken, beans, fried okra, collard greens and corn bread.

'Don't be expectin' to be fed like this on the trail,' Mobley warned with each plateful. 'You'll be lucky to get corn fritters and coffee from now on and any drover that complains can damn well do the cooking hisself.'

They picked out a table and sat down. They were joined by several hands who started introducing themselves.

Boke Yeakly had an outsized Adam's apple that bobbed when he talked and his head was topped by a shock of yellowish unruly hair that had rarely seen a comb. His shirt-tails flapped and his sleeves might or might not have been rolled to equal lengths. While Yeakly had the appearance of an unmade bed, his partner, Jeb Lovelady, with his neatness of dress and close-cropped, tightly curled black hair, gave the impression of careful organization.

They both were from Lampassas County, just over the county line, and had done stock work since the age of thirteen or fourteen. They had worked for Golightly for about ten years, but had never gone on a drive. Lovelady explained their reason for joining the drive.

'We decided to sign on to this drive since it's goin' to be the last one and a short one to boot. We don't want any of that Dakota or Montana business, sittin' on the hurricane deck of a cowpony out in a blizzard. Besides, we kinda have an itch to see Dodge.'

Yeakly grinned a naughtily impish grin while the others chuckled.

Murphy Wheelock, who looked to be at least ten years older than any of the others at the table, said that he grew up on a share-cropping farm in Fannin County. But after his pa died, he said:

'I'd had all the farming I wanted so I lit out on my own. I decided drovin' was preferable to share-cropping. Hell, as far as that goes,' he added, to the chuckles of his dinner companions, "shoveling shit out of old Scratch's stable is better'n sod bustin'.'

As the men talked, Cage noticed that the hand at the far end of the table ignored the conversation, neither looking up to see who spoke nor laughing with the others. Cage assumed that perhaps the man had not eaten for a while and was giving priority to getting the wrinkles smoothed out of his belly before engaging in social discourse. He punched Johnny and nodded toward the loner. Johnny just raised his eyebrows, saying nothing.

Elzee Laroux stood a robust five foot nine and possessed a thick head of black hair and blue eyes. He explained that his people were Cajun but they had come to Texas when he was just a tad.

'We ended up in Texas cause my pa got in a shootin' and cuttin' scrape. But I'm glad we did 'cause if I wadn't here, I'd be squattin' beside a bayou, eatin' crawdads. There's shore 'nuff plenty of opportunities here; I've done farming, drovin', carpentry and even tendin' goats.'

The face he made at his mention of goats brought chuckles from his dinner companions who, as cattlemen, had no use for goats.

'All in all,' Laroux continued, 'I prefer driving cattle, and most of the time the chuck's good.'

He put his arm around the shoulders of a large man sitting next to him.

'This here's Bewley Steiner. I don't know where Bewley's from 'cause he don't know hisself. I ran acrost him in Fort Worth about two years ago. He had been roustaboutin' for some sort of traveling show that went tits up in Fort Worth and they just turned him loose. Since he couldn't remember much about his family, I been lookin' after him ever since.'

Elzee's expression turned serious.

'Now Bewley is slow at some things and he's kinda

innocent of the ways of the world. But he's a damn good worker, he's ox-strong and he can hold his own with anyone with a horse and stock. And nobody's better with animals than he is. Some of you may have noticed that the two of us rode up here on the back of an old mule. Well, that's Bewley's mule and the only transportation available to us when we decided to make the trip here. Old Jenny, as Bewley calls her, wadn't too high on the idea of walking all the way here from San Antone, but Bewley talked to her and kinda reasoned it out with her and here we are.'

Bewley sat with his head down in embarrassment during the recitation, a slight grin curling his lips. He was a big man, standing three inches over six feet. His massive shoulders, thick arms and heavily calloused hands testified to a life of hard labor. Unkempt brownish hair occasionally fell across his forehead. His expression was one of good-natured, childlike innocence. When Elzee told Bewley to say 'hidy' to the boys, Bewley looked up shyly and said 'hidy' then looked down at his plate again.

While the others murmured 'hidy Bewley' or nodded in response, Cage got a glimpse of the loner at the end of the table sneering at Bewley's simple greeting.

When it was his turn, Cage briefly told the group about growing up in Texas but omitted the part about killing Harvey Oleman. He said that he and Johnny had been friends since he'd helped Johnny out in a gunfight after Johnny called a card-cheat's hand.

Johnny seized the opportunity to talk and launched into his story.

'I never knew my ma and I hung around New Orleans with my pa until he died and I lit out and found out there were some pretty interesting places in this country. I spent some time up in Bexar* County and that's where I ran into old Cage here. We been riding together ever since, 'cause old Ben is such a hell-raiser and quim-rustler I have to hang around to keep him from gettin' throwed in jail or gettin' shot by a jealous husband.'

The look on Cage's face told the hands that Johnny was perhaps stretching the truth.

'Just so you know,' Cage added, 'When Johnny tells a story about getting me out of trouble, you can bet money that it was the other way around.'

What Johnny did not tell was that his father had been a professional gambler and Johnny had learned the tricks of the trade at his knee. His father died shot in the back by a poor loser. Johnny inherited a few shirts and an old Colt Navy .45 from his father. He used the .45 to even the score with his father's killer, then fled from New Orleans, never to return.

The group looked expectantly at the hand sitting alone at the end of the table. In the silence, the man looked up to see all eyes on him. He was

*Pronounced BAY er

between twenty-five and thirty years of age and of a nondescript appearance. His height was average and his physique was neither powerful nor scrawny. His face, lacking any sign of character, had no distinguishing features. His eyes were a pale, unfocused blue. It was a face that never would be noticed on the street and, if introduced, forgotten in ten minutes.

'Name's Jarius Welch,' the man muttered, pronouncing the first name ja-*rye*-us. 'From back East. Just a drover.'

With that, Welch turned his attention back to his food. The others exchanged amused glances and shoulder-shrugs and went back to their conversation, which consisted largely of humorous stories of previous drives. Welch ignored the conversation and frequent laughter till his plate was clean, then he left the table and walked outside.

After they had finished off the last of Mobley's chicken and greens, and while the hands were selecting their bunks for their short stay in the bunkhouse, Cage walked outside. He found Welch alone, leaning against a post and smoking a roll-your-own.

'Hidy,' Cage said. 'I'm Benjamin Cage. I understand your name is Jarius?'

Welch turned and looked at Cage, mildly surprised.

'That's right,' he answered.

'Well, Jarius, you didn't look too happy back at

supper. Did somebody say somethin' that rubbed you wrong?'

Welch, taken aback by Cage's frankness, held up a hand, palm outward.

'No, nobody said nothin' to rub me wrong. It's just . . . well, never mind.'

Cage noticed that Welch avoided looking him in the eye while speaking and focused his eyes elsewhere.

Cage was persistent. 'Well, we all are going to be working together to get that herd up to Kansas and I figure that to get the job done, we're going to have to get along with each other.'

Welch was silent. Cage stood waiting for a reply.

Realizing that Cage wasn't going away, Welch eventually answered, fixing his eyes on the far end of the shed.

'It's the dimwit. I don't like dimwits; they're always trouble. This job is hard enough without having to drag around a dimwit.'

'Well, I reckon that if he can't do the job, Matt Stevenson will turn him loose,' said Cage, surprised. 'Besides, Elzee Laroux is going to look after him. I can't see that you're going to be bothered.'

'I hope to hell not,' Welch replied, stamping out the butt of his cigarette. ' 'Bout time to turn in.'

With those words, he turned and walked away.

Before lights-out in the bunkhouse, the hands were sitting and talking in low tones.

Cage leaned close to Johnny's ear. 'I think there's

one bad apple in this barrel,' he whispered. He indicated Welch with a nod of his head.

Johnny glanced at Welch who was bedding down at the far end of the long bunkhouse.

'You noticed it too, huh? I don't like the look outta his eyes, Benjamin,' he said. 'You reckon somethin's wrong with the fellow?'

'Could be,' Cage replied. 'The less we have to do with that *cimarrone** the better. But everybody else seems to be good people. By the way, Elzee told me that Bewley's hire is conditional on Bewley being able to do the job. Golightly says that if he can hold his own with the stock, he's got the job. And he told me something else. If Bewley doesn't get the job, both of them will move on. I reckon he kind of looks after Bewley like he's a little brother.'

'Looks to me like Bewley's pretty lucky,' Johnny observed.

'I hear that,' Cage said, blowing out the lantern.

*An animal that stays apart from the herd.

CHAPTER 2

The next day's activities went as Golightly planned, and Matt Stevenson used the time to closely observe the new hands in action. Any questions he had about Bewley were quickly dispelled. Bewley could throw a hooley-ann* as well as any man he'd ever seen, and when it came to bulldogging, the big man could wrestle a steer to the ground faster than any of the entire crew. At supper that night, Stevenson called Elzee aside and told him that the big man with the child's mind could carry a full workload as well as any of the hands and that he could stay on. Elzee, relieved and delighted, shared the news with Cage.

The next morning, the hands ate breakfast before daybreak in preparation for moving the herd at first light. Cage noticed that Bewley rushed through his breakfast and then disappeared outside.

'Where's Bewley going?' he asked Elzee.

*A short lasso used in close quarters.

17

'He's going to say goodbye to the mule,' Elzee Said, smiling sheepishly. 'Mr Golightly agreed to keep Jenny here and work her some while we were on the trail.'

Bewley returned just before the men mounted up.

'Did you say your goodbyes to Jenny?' Cage asked.

'Yep,' Bewley answered matter-of-factly. 'I had to tell her that we'd be gone for a while but that we'd be back to get her.'

'Did she understand?'

'Sure, and she was kind of glad to have the rest,' Bewley answered. 'I told her that Mr Golightly would have her doing some chores to earn her keep and she thought that was only fair.'

Cage glanced at Elzee who smiled back as if to say, I told you so.

At that moment, Matt Stevenson mounted his horse.

'Let's go to Dodge,' he said.

The weather was still hot in central Texas. Though the day's high temperature still hit the nineties, the hellish, merciless, broiling sun of August had given way to September. The prairie was dry and the 2000 head raised a cloud of dust that made riding drag nothing short of miserable. After a day on drag, a cowboy could put a finger aside his nose and blow a gob of mud out the other side worthy of a dirt-dauber's nest.

The drive had been on the trail for four days when, to no one's surprise, Matt Stevenson named Cage as his *segundo*. The two men were much alike in their dealings with others, and they seemed to share the same level of maturity and thought processes. When Stevenson was absent, scouting ahead or riding into towns along the way for supplies, the change-over in supervision was seamless.

Stevenson had been concerned about Bewley. But as the simple man's reliability became known to all of them, the others worked with him amiably. They became accustomed to his walking into the remuda nearly every night and talking to the horses. Booher, the horse wrangler, reported with some wonder to the others that Bewley actually *did* talk to the horses. Even when the remuda had gone restless over an encounter with a puma, Bewley seemed to have the knack of settling the horses down.

On the thirteenth day, the drive reached the Red River, the border between Texas and Oklahoma. The Big Red had dried to a few trickles between sand bars and the crossing was made without incident. By nightfall, the herd had moved past the lush oak and elm forests that lined the river deep into the open expanse of the Oklahoma Territory. The team bedded the herd down for the night while Mobley started dishing up a supper of pot roast.

After being relieved on watch, Bewley returned

to the chuck wagon ahead of Elzee who was rounding up some strays. Bewley waited patiently for Elzee until Mobley persuaded him to go ahead and eat. Mobley filled his plate and Bewley poured himself a cup of hot coffee from the three-gallon pot hanging over the open fire. There was an old log nearby, the remnants of a fallen tree, and some of the men were seated there, glad of the opportunity to sit instead of squatting to eat their supper. As Bewley moved to join them, Boke Yeakly stood up and bumped the big man's arm. Hot coffee splashed out of Bewley's cup and across Jarius Welch's shoulder.

Welch jumped up screaming in pain. Wild-eyed, he turned on Bewley.

'You goddamned, dimwitted son-of-a-bitch!' he shrieked, 'You burned me! You threw hot coffee all over me! You worthless, stupid bastard!'

Bewley staggered back under the shouts as if struck, confused and still holding the half-empty cup and his plate. Yeakly tried to calm Welch, saying:

'It wasn't his fault, Jarius. I didn't see him and I hit his arm. . . .'

In his fury, Welch ignored Yeakly. He bent down and grabbed a broomstick-sized branch and, swinging it wildly, knocked the coffee-cup from Bewley's hand. Welch started advancing toward Bewley, poking him in the chest with the branch, cursing with each poke. As Welch advanced, Bewley stumbled backwards and stuttered, trying to form words of apology.

Cage, standing twenty feet away, started toward Bewley and his tormentor to stop the fight. Just then, Welch jabbed the branch into Bewley's face and the big man came alive in fury.

'Don't poke my eyes, Jarius!' Bewley yelled. He dropped his supper plate, grabbed Welch's right arm with his left and ripped the branch from Welch's hands. He seized both of Welch's wrists in his enormous hands and squeezed.

Welch's mouth flew open in anguish as Bewley forced the smaller man to his knees. Welch fell to the ground, his body twisting and his legs writhing, trying to dislodge the vice-like grip of Bewley's hands.

'Stop, damn you!' Welch yelled, his voice rising in pitch. 'Somebody stop him!'

'You're a mean man,' Bewley said, his face contorted by rage.

At that moment Cage reached the two, put one hand on Bewley's left arm and the other on his back.

'That's enough Bewley, that's enough,' he said, soothingly. 'He's stopped poking you now. You don't want to break his arms. He won't be able to work.'

Cage repeated the words while gently patting Bewley's back. A flicker of understanding crossed Bewley's face as he turned and looked at Cage.

'Elzee ain't here to tell me what to do, Benjamin.'

Cage continued in a soothing tone: 'If Elzee was here, he'd tell you that the fight is over and to turn him loose.'

Ignoring Welch's cries, Bewley looked at Cage, a puzzled frown on his face. Slowly, the frown relaxed.

'If you say so, Benjamin,' he said, and loosed his grip.

Welch fell to the ground, hugging his arms to his chest, sobbing.

Bewley, almost in tears, asked Cage: 'Where's Elzee?'

'He'll be here in a few minutes, Bewley,' Cage assured him. 'He's rounding up some strays and he'll be here in a few minutes.'

'Jarius is a bad man,' Bewley whispered. 'I got to tell Elzee.'

Cage led Bewley back toward the wagon.

'Are you hungry, Bewley?' Cage asked. 'Let's get you another plate of supper and you can go on and eat and wait for Elzee.'

Welch, feeling each of his wrists alternately to assure himself they weren't broken, shouted at Bewley's back:

'I bet when you popped out, your old man wished he had left your mama alone.'

Bewley spun around at Welch's words, his eyes wild.

'Don't talk about my mama,' he roared, starting toward Welch.

Welch's eyes lit up, he went into a half-crouch and his right hand dropped to his holster. But before he could get the .44 clear of the leather, Cage drew and fired. The shot hit the ground between Welch's feet, throwing up sand. Welch froze, a stunned look on his face.

'Leave that thing in the holster, Welch,' Cage shouted. 'There'll be no killing around here today.'

Welch's hand slowly moved away from the holster. The stunned look changed to fury.

'I won't forget this, Benjamin Cage, you or your damned dimwit friend there,' he said, then turned and walked away.

When the crew turned in that night, the tension in the air was almost tangible. From his bedroll, Johnny whispered to Cage that the men were still talking about his 'lightning draw' and that they figured him for a gunman using the trail drive as cover to hide from the law.

Cage smiled grimly. 'They are darned near right, aren't they? But let 'em think whatever they want to. If some of 'em are scared of me, so much the better. The only problem is that Welch hates my guts now and he strikes me as a back-shooter.'

Johnny chuckled. 'That son-of-a-bitch ought to be grateful you were around when Bewley grabbed him. If you hadn't, he would be walking around with a couple of useless flippers right now.'

Johnny rose up on one elbow so he could see Cage's face by the dim firelight.

'You had Welch figured for trouble before we left Golightly's, didn't you?' he said.

'Yep,' Cage answered. 'And I don't think we've seen the last of the problems yet.'

'Well, good luck to you,' Johnny said. He was silent for a moment then added; 'Hell, I'd better say good luck to all of us.'

CHAPTER 3

They crossed the Red River with ease. The Canadian, however, presented a larger problem.

Stevenson scouted the river and selected a place where the animals would be required to swim the shortest distance. He ordered Mobley's chuck wagon moved across the river first. Five hands tied ropes onto the wagon, three in front and two behind. They moved into the water cautiously, maintaining tension on the front ropes. The two hands behind moved upstream of the wagon so they could keep the rear of the wagon from swinging around in the current. The three hands in front moved into the water cautiously, then carefully maneuvered the wagon's team when their hoofs no longer found solid footing and they had to swim. When the wagon reached the far side safely, the watching hands cheered, and Mobley moved on ahead to set up for supper at the site Stevenson had selected. After hours of swimming, roping and cursing, the hands got the herd across the river with the loss of four head. Both men and animals were spent after the last of the herd reached the far side. Though the sun was still high, Stevenson ordered the herd to be bedded down and gave his men a much-needed rest. The North Canadian, the Cimarron and finally the Arkansas still lay ahead and Stevenson knew the most serious tests of men and horses still awaited them. He conferred with Cage to settle on assignments for the future crossings that would take best advantage of the abilities of the horses and men both had assessed on a daily basis.

Cage and Stevenson were standing by the chuck wagon drinking coffee and making plans when one of the herders cried: 'Injuns!'

Cage and Stevenson looked up to see a band of a half-dozen bucks riding toward them from the east. Stevenson drained the last of the coffee from his tin cup and walked out to meet the Indians. Cage walked out with him and when Stevenson stopped, Cage stopped too, a step behind him and a step to the right. Stevenson turned to the men who were nervously fingering their side arms.

'No guns!' he said. 'Leave 'em in their holsters!' The men glanced at one another and muttered but followed orders.

The bucks rode up and stopped twenty feet from where Stevenson stood. Stevenson raised his right hand, palm outward, in the customary salutation. The oldest of the Indians, who seemed to be in charge, returned the salute, then slid down from the bare back of his pony. He carried a Winchester 73 that appeared to be in good condition. One other member of his party carried a firearm: what appeared to be an old Sharps rifle. The others carried spears, decorated with eagle-feathers, or bows and a skin quiver full of arrows.

The chief spoke to Stevenson in a language that Cage didn't understand, turning and pointing at the herd. Stevenson shook his head and answered in the same tongue, holding up two fingers. The old man spoke gruffly, a note of threat in his voice, and held up six fingers. Cage glanced back at the men. They were standing stock-still and wide-eyed, watching the proceedings with some apprehension. The other bucks watched the cowboys warily from the backs of their ponies.

The exchange between Stevenson and the chief went on for another five minutes, each shaking his head and answering the other in what seemed to Cage to be growls. Eventually they both nodded and the tone of their voices grew softer. They had reached an agreement. The chief turned to his men and spoke. The braves quickly dismounted.

Stevenson turned to Cage.

'They wanted six beeves to take back with them,' he said. 'I told them no but they could have two. We argued a bit and finally agreed on three head of their choice. On top of that, we feed 'em supper.'

Then to Mobley he said: 'The braves are going to

have supper with us, Mobley. I think your beef stew smelled good to them.'

Mobley got out more tin plates and served stew to the Indians and gave each of them two biscuits. The braves were obviously hungry and ate quickly with their hands. As they squatted there, some of the drovers quietly moved away. When a breeze wafted the scent of the seven red men to Cage's nostrils, he realized why the men had been putting a few more yards between themselves and their guests. The Indians had a sharp odor about them, something akin to that of a fox but more pungent.

'Who are these folks?' Boke asked Stevenson.

Stevenson smiled. 'They live on a reservation not far from here and were out foraging for game or whatever they could turn up. I don't think the Indian agents in charge of the reservation allow them to overeat.'

The men chuckled.

Stevenson continued: 'They call themselves "Minumu". The Spaniards called them "Comanche".'

At that, the men looked upon their dinner guests with considerably more respect.

When the meal was finished, the braves got to their feet and without a word, remounted their ponies. The chief said something to Stevenson, then the six dashed away toward the herd. In minutes, they had cut out three of the best looking beeves and, with wild whoops, drove them away in the direction from where they had come.

The men watched them out of sight, and then Boke spoke up.

'Those fellows were considerable whiffy on the downwind side.'

As the laughter died, Stevenson said; 'I'll lay money they are saying the same thing about us right now.'

'How come you let those savages have any of our stock at all?'

Everyone turned toward the speaker. It was Welch.

Stevenson raised an eyebrow. 'Worried about your bonus, are you?'

'Yeh, sure,' Welch answered.

Stevenson glanced at the other men. Most looked embarrassed that the question had been asked.

'Don't worry about it,' he said with a slight smile. 'We brought along enough head to make up for those that die or drown in the river crossings or that we give to the Indians. We'll make our count. Three head is a cheap enough price to make sure we don't get rustled at night or have to shoot a brave.' He paused and his eyes swept across the faces of the men. 'And it's plenty cheap enough to let some brave men who have lost about everything else to hang on to some dignity.'

Some of the men nodded in agreement and the crowd broke up, some to eat their supper and others to return to their posts.

Johnny sidled up to Cage.

'Well danged if that Welch ain't the most lovable drover in the bunch,' he whispered.

Cage laughed and got in line for his stew.

The Golightly herd had been on the trail for three weeks and Cage was in charge. Matt Stevenson had ridden ahead to scout for a crossing-place on the Canadian River, a milestone they expected to reach in another day. In late afternoon, the riders could see clouds building in the west and the feel of the air told them that their prospect for thunderstorms before morning was almost certain. They bedded down the herd for the night in pasture between a thick stand of timber on one side and an overgrown creek on the other. Cage was apprehensive about the prospects of a thunderstorm coming upon them during the night and spooking the herd. He doubled the night watch and divided up his hands into two-hour guards, cautioning them to be alert for anything.

Elzee, Bewley, Jeb, Will and two others drew the two o'clock to four duty and reluctantly climbed out of their blanket rolls, donned their oilcloth ponchos and mounted up at the appointed hour, greeted by flashes of lightning and distant thunder.

They took their places and relieved the midnight-to-two riders, who were happy to get back to camp before the rain hit. Elzee, Bewley and Murphy took the perimeter that bordered on the creek while Cage and the others took the side that backed up to the dense stand of trees. Cage rode up to the north edge, placing himself between the herd and the path they were to take the next day. The animals were becoming restive due to the nearing flashes of lightning and accompanying rolls of thunder. As a precaution, he rode back to the camp, rousted out the others and returned to the north end of the pasture.

As the additional riders took their places, barely a hundred yards into the timber at the tail end of the herd, an enormous lightning bolt sizzled into the top of a tree with a sharp-edged crash. Boke Yeakly's mount, spooked by the lightning, reared and bucked. The beeves on that side, already nervous, were set off by the sound and the horse's agitation, and surged away from the disturbance into the herd. Yeakly had his horse under control in seconds, but the damage had been done.

Panic spread through the herd almost instantly and it surged west and to the north toward Elzee and Bewley almost as a single organism. Cage and the others spurred their mounts to a gallop, trying to reach the lead animals. In a moment, the herd spilled out at the north end of the pasture and began gaining speed up the trail.

At that moment the heavens seemed to open and release a downpour accompanied by almost contin-uous flashes of lightning. Totally out of control, the herd raced north at top speed.

Cage spurred his mount unmercifully and raced

alongside the herd, slowly gaining ground. As he approached the lead animals, lightning flashes revealed Johnny on the other side of the frantic mob with another rider close behind. At last the three met, a dozen yards ahead of the pack, and Cage motioned to his left toward an open expanse of ground. The three drew along the right side of the lead animals and started firing into the air. At first, the stubborn brutes resisted turning, but after Cage neared the lead animal, almost close enough to touch, and fired two shots into the ground close to his head, the crazed brute veered to the left, followed by the animals in his wake. True to their nature, the rest of the herd followed.

The riders stayed close to the lead and kept the lead animals veering left. When the end of the herd approached, the leads merged into the tail end of the stampede.

Several riders had joined them during the dash and rode the outskirts of the mob until the pace slowed and the herd milled aimlessly till the cause for their flight was forgotten. The hands kept patrolling the edges of the herd keeping the animals milling until the lightning trailed off in the distance and calm returned.

As the sky lightened in the east, Cage dispatched four riders to search for strays that might have become separated from the herd during the head-long rush. He stood in his stirrups and counted the remaining riders.

'We're short one,' he said.

The riders looked at one another and at the riders on the other side of the herd to determine who was missing.

'Where's Bewley?' Elzee exclaimed, failing to see him among those riding the herd's perimeter.

With concern wrinkling his brow, Cage said: 'Elzee, ride back along the trail and see if you can spot him. His horse may have gone lame.'

Elzee spurred his mount into a lope and headed south along the trail over which the herd had rampaged. He was amazed at how far the herd had traveled during its headlong flight. During the stampede, he had thought they traveled only a short distance but realized that they had ridden what must have been four miles before getting the herd under control. There was no sign of Bewley until Elzee neared the meadow where the stampede had started. In the dim light he saw what appeared to be a mound of earth in the middle of the muddy trail churned up by thousands of hoofs. As he grew closer, panic rose in his stomach because he could see what looked like a half-dozen beeves that had fallen, then had been flattened by the stampeding herd. Slowing his mount to a walk, he could see the carcass of what had been a horse lying just the other side of the dead cattle and worse, he could make out a yellow poncho in the churned earth near the horse.

Elzee stopped, dismounted, fell to his knees and retched violently.

When Cage rode up beside him, Elzee was kneeling on the wet ground, sobbing. Cage rode slowly to the place where the small patch of yellow was visible. Then he turned his horse and told Elzee to stay with the body and rode back to notify the others.

Cage sent two hands back to the chuck wagon for canvas and shovels. Using the shovels, Boke and Jeb undertook to extricate Bewley's body from the mud with which it mingled. They wrapped the body, which no longer resembled a human, in the canvas and carried to the edge of the trees.

Matt Stevenson returned while the grave was being dug under a towering oak tree and Cage filled him in on the night's events.

One of the riders carved 'Bewley Steiner' on the trunk. No one knew his date of birth, so only his date of death appeared under the name.

The service over Bewley was a simple one. Matt Stevenson read passages from his Bible, then spoke of the dead man.

'We are all going to miss Bewley. We are going to miss his kindness, his simple ways and his love of animals. There's an old mule back in Texas that's going to miss him a lot when he doesn't come back for her.'

He bowed his head and said, 'Let us pray. Lord, we ask you to have mercy on the soul of a poor cowboy who never had an evil thought, who was kind to everyone. We also ask that you comfort Bewley's friend, Elzee Laroux, who gave of himself to take care of another of your children who needed someone to look after him. We ask that you watch over us and keep the rest of us from harm.'

Those who knew it recited the Lord's Prayer. After the 'Amen', Elzee and Murphy Wheelock started filling the grave while the other riders returned to their mounts in preparation for moving out.

Johnny looked back at the grave. 'I don't want to be buried on the trail and forgotten,' he said. 'I want a headstone and my family there to mourn for me.'

'It sounds like you've made a decision,' Cage said.

'I have,' Johnny said firmly. 'This is my last drive.'

After the grave was filled, Elzee and Murphy returned the shovels to the chuck wagon and mounted up. The herd started moving northward once again.

CHAPTER 4

The last day on the trail they had to cross the Arkansas. While Cage was haltering the horse he knew as the best swimmer, Elzee approached him.

'Ben, I want to talk to you about Welch.'

'What's that, Elzee?'

'Do you think anything was peculiar about the way that Bewley died?'

Cage turned and looked at Elzee.

'Peculiar? You mean you think maybe Welch was responsible?'

Elzee hesitated, thinking.

'It's just that Welch had the opportunity. I was an eighth of a mile in front of Bewley and Welch was back there somewhere. It wouldn't have been much of a problem during the stampede with that storm going on to ride up and shoot Bewley or maybe his horse. No one would have paid any attention to the shot because it would have been just one more in forty or fifty.'

'I suppose what you're saying is possible, Elzee.

But how are you ever going to prove it? Anyone who would hear about how Bewley died would just figure his mount turned the cat.'

'I know I can't prove it,' Elzee answered. 'But it's too much of a happenstance. All I can say is that that son-of-a-bitch Welch had better watch his ass from now on because I'm goin' to be watching every move he makes.'

'If you learn anything, let me know,' Cage said.

Watching Elzee ride away, he knew Elzee's grief had given way to anger. One problem had gone away and another had taken its place, he mused grimly.

The riders set to work getting the herd across the Arkansas. They had had heavy experience working with one another by this time and they had a good crossing, losing two head. When the river was at last behind them, Stevenson directed the herd to a wide, level stretch near a creek where water was plentiful and there was enough grazing to keep the herd quiet. Posting four men to watch the herd, he gave the others leave to visit Dodge City and offered to make a modest advance toward their final pay for anyone who needed it.

Johnny and the others wasted no time in digging out their best clothes and, with wild whoops, rode at top speed toward what the Eastern newspapers called 'Gomorrah on the Arkansas', Dodge City. Cage made certain that the herd was safely bedded down and that he wasn't to be needed for a few hours, then he prepared to follow his friends. Stevenson told him that Golightly had made the trip by train to be there to close the sale and pay off the men and wanted to meet the both of them at Delmonico's for dinner at eight o'clock.

Arriving in town, Cage found a stable that would put up his horse for twenty-five cents and since Dodge City lawmen would not allow arms to be carried in town, he stored his sidearm in a lock-up right there on the premises. He sought out a barbershop that offered hot baths, washed the trail dust off and donned clean clothes. Shortly afterward he found Johnny and Murphy at the Yellow Bird saloon where they each pointed and laughed at one another with faces 'smooth as a baby's butt'. After taking refreshments, they moved on down the street to another establishment, called 'Rotary Rosie's', which offered diversions such as faro and poker, not to mention ladies of easy virtue.

While Johnny was engaged in a game of faro, Murphy wandered on down the street and Cage stood at the bar and sipped a beer. Suddenly, he felt a tug at his elbow and turned to face what must have been the most superannuated whore in Rosie's stable. She had attempted to dye her hair red but the resulting color fell nearer that of an out-of-control forest fire than authentic red hair. To compensate for the pallor of her skin, the wretched creature had been too generous with the rouge on her cheeks and mouth with the result resembling a wrinkled circus clown. Her shriveled lips flapped when she talked because of the total absence of teeth. Her arms were draped in loose folds of flesh.

Before Cage had a chance to react, the old crone launched into her sales pitch.

'Hello there, sweetie. Look's like you're a little lonesome. How about spending a little time with old Sally. You look like you've been out on the range for a while and I bet you're looking for something to calm your nerves.'

Cage tried to move away but Sal grabbed his sleeve and cornered him against the bar.

'I tell you what, sweetie, you being so young and pretty and all, old Sal will give you a straight Frenchie for just a dollar.'

Cage eased away.

To reassure him, Sal played her trump card.

'I guarantee it'll be better than any of that wooly booger you're going to find around here. You won't catch any crabs and you don't even have to take your pants off.'

Cage looked again at that toothless maw surrounded by shriveled, painted lips and pulled his arm out of her grip.

'It'll be the best you ever had, sweetie, and just because I like you I'll cut the price to six bits. How's that?'

But at that point, old Sal was talking to Cage's back as he moved rapidly toward the door. He burst through the swinging doors and down the boardwalk for several feet before looking back. Toothless Sal was not in pursuit but Jeb Lovelady and Boke Yeakly were. Both were laughing so hard they could hardly stand.

'I never seen you move so fast, Benjamin Cage,' Boke exclaimed, his Adam's apple bobbing furiously. 'You'd think old Scratch hisself was after you.' More laughter. 'You shouda' seen your face. That was better'n a freak show.'

Cage, with a grim smile, stood waiting for the pair's hilarity to die down.

'We was watchin' you standin' at the bar, sippin' that beer and lookin' wise as a tree full of owls,' Jeb added. 'We thought you needed company so we told old Gummy Sal you had been on the range for three months and were hornier than a two-peckered billy-goat.' More laughter.

Cage thought about that withered mouth and toothless smile and shuddered.

'Well, you fellows really got my goat this time, I have to admit.'

'You mighty right 'bout that,' Boke bragged. 'Problem is that you don't hardly ever do nothin' that let nobody git yer goat. You's always proper as a old schoolmarm.'

'But we got a story to tell now,' Jeb announced. 'How old Cage got caught talkin' up old Gummy Sal.'

Both Boke and Ben again dissolved into laughter.

'I'll tell you what, citizens,' Cage said. 'Since I

don't care to get close enough to old Gummy Sal to smell her breath a second time, I'm going to this place next door and have a beer. You can tell Johnny to come get me there when he's finished throwin' his money away.'

More laughter.

'We'll do that,' Jeb agreed. 'Jes' make sure you don't fall into the clutches of one of those evil old gals in there.'

The two turned and disappeared through the door of Rotary Rosie's and Cage walked down to the next pair of swinging doors, the Dodge Dance Hall. He found that he could buy a beer and watch or he could buy tickets at two for twenty-five cents that allowed him dance with any available hostess. He decided to listen to the music and watch the dancers. He sat down at an empty table.

Some of the trail hands, inhibitions lowered by whiskey and the spirit of the occasion, improvised wild dance steps to the amusement of friends and onlookers. Others were content to approximate rhythmic movements with feet more accustomed to the stirrup than the intricacies of the dance floor.

The hostesses were clad in yellow-and-black costumes cut low in front to better display inviting bosoms while multiple petticoats bolstered their skirts. Three large men wearing black denims, white shirts and string ties and carrying truncheons kept a close eye on the dancers. Those patrons who felt they should realize a more substantial benefit from the purchase of tickets and attempted to fondle their partners were quickly reminded of the rules of the establishment. One such cowboy who became belligerent upon being admonished by one of the bouncers was rapped lightly on the head and escorted to the door by two of the guardians with his legs resembling India rubber.

The music had stopped momentarily when Cage heard a feminine voice say: 'You look kinda lonely, cowboy. Want company?'

Expecting to see another horror like Gummy Sal, Cage looked up and was surprised to see that the speaker was a pretty young girl of about eighteen. Because of her youth, her profession had not yet begun to erode her natural beauty. A heart-shaped face gave her an air of innocence and her skin still had the blush of youth. Her hair, on its way to turning dark, was still predominantly blond. Her eyes were blue and clear and seemed to shine in the light of the lanterns that hung overhead. 'Well, what do you say?' she asked, her eyes growing wide.

Cage rose to his feet and pulled out a chair.

'Please sit down,' he said.

'Just for a minute,' she cautioned. 'They won't let us sit and gab while the music's playing unless you buy a ticket. You can get them over there, two for two bits. My name's Nancy by the way.'

'Howdy, Nancy,' Cage said. 'I'm Benjamin Cage. I'll be right back.' He walked to the booth where the tickets were sold and bought fifty cents' worth.

Most women thought Cage to be handsome but since he had reached his mid-twenties, some found him a bit disquieting. The coolly appraising gaze from those deep-set eyes was too penetrating, too personal. But he found that those who longed for adventure or were aroused by a hint of danger seemed to be drawn to him.

When he returned to the table, Nancy was talking to another patron who held several tickets in his hand.

'I'm sorry,' she was saying, 'but this gentlemen right here already spoke for me and he's got,' she glanced at Cage's hand, 'four tickets.'

The cowhand looked sour and turned away.

'I'm glad you got back, he smelled bad,' she said, giggling and wrinkling her nose. 'Do you want to dance or just talk?'

'I think I'd prefer to talk,' Cage answered.

They exchanged information about where they were from and Nancy told him about her parents who were poor farmers who were trying to make ends meet and about how she came to Dodge and started work in the dance hall so she could send some money home. As she talked, Cage was reminded of Sophie back home. He hadn't seen her in a while and he wondered if she had taken up with anyone. Like Nancy, she was bright-eyed, innocent and optimistic, still expecting the most out of life. Though he wasn't that much older, he had acquired a bone-deep cynicism in his twenty-five years that made the difference in his and Nancy's ages seem wide as the Llano Estacado.

'See that dark-haired girl over there?' she asked, pointing at a pretty girl dancing with a tall cowboy. 'That's Mary Ann. Most of the girls live in Dodge, but me and Mary Ann don't have any folks here so we share a room out back to keep expenses down. Mr Kirby, the man who owns the dance hall, rents it to us. Mary Ann has a beau who comes to visit her. But she's awful nice and it's good to have someone to talk to.'

'You don't have a beau?' Cage asked.

'No, I don't,' she answered. 'It's sort of hard workin' in a place like this to meet someone that you'd want to get to know better. Most of the fellows are just passin' through and want to have a good time while they're here. Most of 'em drink a lot too. You don't seem to drink much and you sure don't cuss any.'

Cage chuckled. 'There's a reason for that. My pa said there's no call for cussing in front of decent folks. He would have slapped me up the side of the head if 1 ever cussed in front of a lady.'

'I think I would have liked your pa,' she said.

Cage bought more tickets and they talked until Cage had to leave for his dinner appointment. Nancy got up from her chair and stood on tiptoes to kiss Cage on the cheek.

'I've loved talking to you. You're so very nice. Would you like to come back tonight after I get off?'

Cage hesitated a moment, then answered: 'Yes, I would like that.'

'Come by at eleven thirty, and we can go somewhere and talk some more,' she said, smiling.

'I'll be here,' he said.

At the door, he looked back. A cowboy with dance tickets in his hand was talking to Nancy. He also glanced at the table in the dim far corner of the dance hall where Jarius Welch sat, watching Nancy just as he had been for the last hour.

CHAPTER 5

Stevenson and Golightly were pleasant dinner companions. Golightly was an educated and well-read man who kept up with Texas's bizarre politics. He said that the prohibitionists were gaining strength in Texas and that it was possible that one day a man wouldn't be able to buy a drink of whiskey anywhere in the state. Stevenson observed, to Golightly's and Cage's amusement, that when all the saloons closed up, there were an awful lot of cowboys, muleskinners and idlers who would have to take up needlepoint to pass the time.

After the meal, Golightly got around to the purpose of the get-together.

'Cage, I understand from Stevenson here that you are as good a trail boss as a man could find anywhere,' Golightly said. 'And not only that, you're a damn sight smarter than most of 'em.'

'I appreciate the compliment, Mr Golightly,' Cage answered.

'Times are changing in the cattle business, Cage,'

Golightly went on. 'I plan to semi-retire soon and turn most of the business over to Stevenson. But I need another man I can rely on and I wanted to see if you were interested.'

Cage was silent for a moment then decided his answer would need a full explanation.

'Gentlemen,' he said, ' I have been marking time before returning to my home town and trying to start all over there. I left there two years ago because I had to kill someone. This person was doing something crooked and I called him on it. It's a long story so I won't go into it, but we ended up drawing down on one another and I got the best of it. This fellow that I killed was very popular and had a lot of followers. Though the law exonerated me, I was an outcast. This drive was to be the last one for Johnny and me. We are going back to Blackstone and see how things stand. If things don't work out, and I don't stay in Blackstone, can I give you a holler?'

Golightly said he'd be happy to hear from him.

When the dinner broke up, Cage walked out onto the boardwalk in front of the restaurant and was surprised to see Johnny and Elzee walking toward him.

'Ben, you got to hear what Jarius has been up to,' said Johnny. 'He's sure 'nough a strange bird. I brought Elzee up here to tell you.'

'I've spent the afternoon cold-trailing Welch,' Elzee said in the way of explanation.

'What did you find out?' Cage asked.

Elzee drew his two friends out of the foot traffic to the edge of the boardwalk to tell his tale.

'This afternoon, I follow him down here to the main part of town and I figure he's going to get hisself a drink of whiskey and a woman. But instead of goin' in a saloon, he goes around back and walks down an alley. Now I'm trying to keep from bein' seen and it ain't easy in broad daylight, but I got into a horse barn where I could see him through the cracks between the boards. He was wearing a yellow shirt so he was easy to track. You know that stretch where the Trail Drive saloon and Rotary Rosie's and that dance hall next to it is?'

'Yeh, we know those places,' Johnny answered.

'Well,' Elzee continued, 'he stops in back of that dance hall and looks up at a landin' on the back of the building where there's what looks like rooms. At least there's doors and windows. I don't know who uses those rooms, maybe whores for all I know, but he sure was interested in 'em. Then he goes to the back door of that dance hall and opens it up and takes a quick look inside. After that, he walks away and gets his horse and rides off. And that's about it, but I'm wonderin' why a trail herder is so curious about somethin' that don't concern 'im.'

As Elzee talked, Cage grew uneasy. He knew that Nancy and Mary Ann shared a room 'in back' of the dance hall.

'I don't like the smell of that,' he said. 'I think I'll just mosey on down to the dance hall.'

'You go on,' Johnny said. 'I'll know where to find you.'

Cage walked briskly down the boardwalk toward the dance hall. Too much of a coincidence, he muttered to himself, knowing that Welch's interest in the dance hall was more than idle curiosity.

Reaching the dance hall, he shoved through the swinging doors and stopped to survey the room, looking for Nancy. When he couldn't see her on the dance floor, he walked the perimeter of the big room vainly hoping to find her at a table chatting with a range hand. Just then, the music stopped and he saw Mary Ann being released from the grasp of a trail hand and pausing to catch her breath.

'Mary Ann, have you seen Nancy?' Cage asked.

Mary Ann looked puzzled, then her face brightened.

'You must be Ben,' she trilled. 'Nancy told me about you.'

'That's right and I'm looking for Nancy.'

Mary Ann frowned. 'She's not here. She went to meet you. That cowboy that come in here a while ago said that you was in trouble and needed to see her.'

Cage's mouth tightened. 'What cowboy? What did he look like?'

'I don't know,' Mary Ann whimpered, intimidated by Cage's manner. 'He didn't look like anything in particular. But he was wearing a yellow shirt.'

Cage grabbed both of a frightened Mary Ann's arms.

'Which room is the one you share with Nancy?'

'The last one at the top of the stairs,' Mary Ann blurted, her eyes wide.

Cage turned and walked quickly to the back door. Shoving the door open, he saw a flight of stairs on his left. He took the stairs in five bounds. Three rooms, each with a window, opened onto the landing, and he went immediately to the last one. The curtains were drawn, but there was a lantern burning in the room. He could hear what sounded like moans. He tried the knob but the door was locked from the inside. He leaned back and kicked the door, shattering the lock.

The door slammed open on a scene of horror. Jarius Welch was on his knees on one of the two beds in the room. He was naked, splattered with blood and kneeling astride Nancy's bloody body. The blood had poured out of her slashed throat. Her eyes were still open and her mouth gaped as if in surprise at what was being done to her. Welch was holding his erect penis in his blood-soaked right hand.

Cage stood as if frozen, stunned by the nightmarish scene. Welch turned and stared at Cage with glazed eyes. He suddenly came awake and cast about frantically until he saw the knife on the floor by the bed where he had dropped it. Before Welch could dive off the bed to retrieve the knife, Cage, with a cry of rage, charged into the room and hit him in the side of the head with a straight right. Welch fell backward off the bed onto the floor where his clothes were piled. Scrambling among the clothes, Welch pulled out a pistol. Before Welch could swing the gun around to fire, Cage leaped across the bed and fell on him, grabbing his wrist and throat. The pistol fired but the bullet went into the ceiling. At that moment, there was a horrible scream from the doorway. Mary Ann stood horrified at the ghastly wreckage of the girl who had been her friend. She screamed again and again.

Welch was surprisingly strong and he attempted to swing the pistol's barrel around to bear on his adversary's face, thumbing the hammer back. Cage grabbed the top of the pistol with his left hand, forcing the fleshy web at the base of his thumb under the hammer. Welch squeezed the trigger but the hammer cut into the flesh of Cage's hand instead of the primer. Pinning Welch's right hand and the pistol to the floor with his left hand, Cage released Welch's throat and smashed his rock-hard fist into his jaw. Cage hit him again and Welch fell unconscious.

Cage took the pistol from Welch's limp hand and pulled the hammer back, releasing his hand. He turned and looked at the body of the young girl with the sparkling eyes then back at the unconscious man.

'You crazy pile of shit!' he roared and took

Welch's throat in his hands, intending to crush it.

Suddenly, there was a hand on his shoulder. 'Hold it cowboy,' a voice said. 'We'll let the hangman take care of that.'

Ben turned to see a deputy marshal standing over him. Reluctantly he took his hands from the blood-smeared throat.

City Marshal Joshua Webb was summoned and took Welch into custody. The sight in the girls' bedroom shook even that veteran lawman and he covered the body with a sheet from the other bed. His two deputies, ashen-faced, yanked the semi-conscious Welch to his feet, manacled his hands, pulled his trousers on and carried the blood-covered man away to the city jail. A fainting Mary Ann had already been led away from the scene by two of the dance-hall girls. Marshal Webb asked Cage to come to his office and make a statement.

Webb sat behind his desk and poured a shot of whiskey from a bottle kept in the desk drawer. Cage rarely drank whiskey but he welcomed the heat of the liquid and its calming effect. One of the deputies poured a bit of coal-oil on the small wound in Cage's hand which the firing-pin of Welch's gun had left.

Cage gave the marshal a concise report on his discovery of the crime and his actions. He included in his statement the suspicions of some of his friends on the trail drive that Welch might have had something to do with Bewley Steiner's death during a stampede.

The marshal eventually said that he had enough information for the present time and told Cage to go, after cautioning him that he would have to be a witness at the trial, which would be arranged as quickly as possible. As Cage walked out, he met an unusually somber Johnny. The two collected their horses and side-arms and rode back to the cow camp in silence.

The next morning, the crew moved Golightly's herd to the pens where Matt Stevenson and the buyer counted the animals. When they agreed on a final count of 2014 head and the transaction was completed, Stevenson set up a field desk and paid off the hands. Then he made a trip to the jail to leave Welch's pay with the marshal. After saying their goodbyes, the crew started to disperse to their various destinations. Cage and Johnny found that Elzee planned to stay until Welch's trial was over and the three of them found a room on the outskirts of town which, while far from luxurious, would suit their needs until they could leave Dodge for good.

That night, as the three of them tried to settle in for sleep, Johnny said:

'Well, Ben, I reckon you shoulda shot Welch when you had the chance instead of just dustin' his boots.'

'I suppose so, Johnny,' Cage answered. 'Two

decent people are dead now who would still be alive if I had. But that's "should have" talk. When someone is drawing a six-gun, there's no time to ponder. What you have to do is the thing that is instinctive at that split second.'

Cage paused for a moment.

'Now it comes back to me,' he said. 'The look on Welch's face that night around the fire. Johnny, remember when you were telling about us messing around in Fort Worth and you told the fellows about Karalou?'

'Yeh, I remember.'

'I happened to look at Welch when you were describing Karalou. I didn't understand then, that look he had. I didn't understand because he wasn't an ordinary man thinking about a pretty girl, he was thinking of things right out of hell.'

The three of them were silent for a long while.

'The problem with a split second decision,' Cage said at last, 'is you go to bed every night for the rest of your life with it, good or bad.'

Elzee said 'Amen' and turned out the lantern.

The next day, Cage learned that justice moved swiftly in Dodge City and the trial was scheduled for the fourth day after the murder. The day before the trial was to start, he went to Marshal Webb's office. The marshal welcomed him and poured a cup of coffee.

'What can I do for you, Cage?' the marshal asked.

Cage frowned and sipped at his coffee.

'I was wondering if you had learned anything

from Welch that might cast some light on why he did what he did.'

The marshal smiled and looked at Cage.

'Well, I have and I haven't. What I have learned is that the marshal of a town like this ain't up to figuring out what I do know. I think it would take one of them alienist doctors from back East to make heads or tails of it.'

'Why's that, Marshal?'

'He won't say where he's from or even what his real name is. But what I found out was that when he was little, he had some problems at home.'

'What kind of problems?'

'He had an older brother that used to do things to him. As far as I can tell, the brother used to bugger him on a regular basis.'

'Good God!' Cage exclaimed. 'What were the parents doing while this was going on?'

'I don't know for sure, maybe didn't believe him when he complained, or didn't care. Some kind of poor white trash, suppose. But the thing is . . . the brother was a dimwit.'

'So that was it,' Cage said under his breath.

The marshal smiled grimly.

'Thought that might ring some kind of bell from what you fellows told me about that boy that got killed on the drive.'

'It sure does, Marshal. But I suppose we'll never know for sure. Did you ask him about Bewley Steiner?'

'Yep, sure did. But he wouldn't talk, just kind of smiled in that funny way of his. By the way, another thing I couldn't get is what happened at home before he left. All he'd say is, "I put it right".'

'You think he got even with the brother?' Cage asked.

The marshal leaned back in his chair and squinted at Cage.

'I've been in this business for close on twenty years,' he said. 'I've questioned a lot of people, good and bad and the bad ones were as bad as they come. After so long, you get a feel for things, you sort of know what the answer is before they give it. Cage, I'd give you eight to five odds that he killed all three of them.'

'Marshal,' Cage said, smiling, 'after what I've seen him do, I don't think I'd take that bet.'

When the trial started, the defense attorney whom Welch hired with his trail pay objected that he had not had sufficient time to prepare his case, but the judge overruled him.

The trial went swiftly, as was expected. After the other prosecution witnesses testified, Cage was called to the stand. The prosecutor asked about why he went to the room in back of the dance hall, then asked him to describe what he saw after he kicked the door open.

Cage told his story in a measured voice.

'When I kicked the door open, I saw Jarius Welch

on the bed, kneeling astraddle the body. Nancy's throat had been cut and her body was cut up some.'

'What was the defendant wearing?'

'Nothing. He was naked.'

'What was he doing there astraddle the body?'

'He had his male member in his right hand.'

'What was he doing with his male member?'

'He was lopin' it.'

'Loping it? You mean he was masturbating.'

'Yessir, that's what he appeared to be doing.'

'What was he doing with his left hand?'

'He was holding something bloody. I didn't know what it was at that time but later I found out it was Nancy's left breast.'

There was a disturbance in the courtroom as a lady spectator fainted.

At that moment, the looks of horror on the jurors' faces sealed Welch's fate.

The jury deliberated fifteen minutes and returned a verdict of murder in the first degree.

The judge sentenced Welch to hang.

Out on the boardwalk, the prosecutor shook Cage's hand and thanked him for his straightforward testimony.

The three companions returned to their hotel and made plans to leave the next morning. Elzee said he was planning to stay in Dodge until he could watch Welch hang, then he was heading for Tennessee where he had some relatives and might perhaps find a steady job, adding that he had had enough of trail drives. Johnny told him that he and Ben were heading for Blackstone, Texas.

'If you need to reach us, just write in care of the town marshal,' Cage said. 'The letter will get to us.'

'You planning on being in gaol?' Elzee asked.

'No, the town marshal is my uncle,' Cage explained.

That night, Johnny grew restless and decided he had to go into Dodge for one last hand of faro.

'I think I'll ride in with you,' said Cage.

When they reached town, Johnny headed for Rotary Rosie's while Cage turned his steps toward the jail. When he walked in the front door, the deputy on duty looked up in surprise.

'Well now, Mr Cage,' he said. 'I sure didn't expect to see you here.'

'I wanted to see if I could have a word with Jarius Welch.'

The deputy squinted his eyes as if trying to remember something.

'Since the trial is over,' he mused, 'you're no longer a witness, so's I calculate it don't make no difference, one way or t' other.' He picked up a ring of keys. 'Foller me,' he said.

Welch lay on his back on the narrow bunk which was the sole furnishing of the cell he occupied. His left arm was over his eyes, shading them from the lantern that illuminated the hallway.

'You got company, Jarius,' the deputy said in a wheedling tone. Then to Cage he said: 'Take all the time you need. He ain't goin' nowhere. Rap on the door when you're ready.'

Welch kept the arm over his eyes. He was silent for a moment then said: 'Couldn't stay away, eh Cage?'

Cage felt a shiver go through his body when Welch spoke his name.

'How'd you know it was me, Jarius?'

'Who else would it be?'

Jarius sat up on the edge of the bed and looked at his visitor.

'Come by to say "hidy" or just to gloat?'

'I just came by to ask you why you picked Nancy,' said Cage. 'Of all the women in this town, you picked her. Why?'

Welch fixed him with unblinking pale-blue eyes.

'Because she was a "nice" girl. You knew that didn't you? I was wondering which one it would be 'cause I'd already settled on that place there. It was just right. I had talked to her and Mary Ann and some of the others and I was waiting for the voice in my head to tell me which one. Then in comes who else but straight arrow Ben Cage who wouldn't say "shit" if he fell through the outhouse floor. Mister fast-draw, righteous fucking Ben Cage. When I saw you two mewling over each other, I knew she was the one.'

'I don't understand,' Cage said, frowning.

'The whores are no fun is what I'm saying; they're ugly and nasty and doomed to hell anyway,' Welch explained, his eyes wide. 'It's got to be one that's nearest the angels. I knew if I watched you, you'd find just what I was looking for.'

Welch jumped off the bed and grabbed the bars, laughing. Cage had never heard Welch laugh. It was as much sob as laugh.

Grasping the bars, Welch pushed his face between two of them.

'If no one cared about those girls, it wouldn't be no good,' he rasped. 'Just remember, you was the one that picked her.'

Cage was silent for what seemed a long time. 'I'm sorry about whatever made you this way, Jarius. That's why I came here to see you, just to tell you that. And I'm sorry that I had to be the one to find you out and send you to the gallows.'

'Well, ain't that sweet,' Welch said sarcastically. 'But I ain't standing under that gallows yet, mister.'

Welch's eyes cut briefly to the next cell.

'I better go,' Cage said wearily, starting toward the door.

'Before you go,' Jarius whispered, 'I just want to tell you that you'll pay for showin' up early that evening. You wadn't 'sposed to show up until late that night.'

Cage turned, surprised.

Welch grinned at the look on Cage's face.

'Oh yeah, I knew about your little rendezvous for that night. It was easy enough to find out. Those girls talk to each other all the time, 'specially about their gentleman callers. And another thing, that was some show you put on back there in that court-room. You'll pay for that too, Cage.'

Cage turned, puzzled.

'If it's the last thing I do,' continued Welch in a rasping whisper, 'I'll find you and I'll make you suffer. Mark my words, holy mouth, high and mighty Ben Cage. Sooner or later, I'll find you and what I did to your sweet little Nancy won't hold a candle to what I got planned for everyone you hold dear. And don't you forget it.'

Cage shook his head, smiling grimly.

'You're raving, just raving, Jarius. They're goin' to hang you,' he said, matter-of-factly. 'You won't be getting back at me or anyone else.'

Again, Jarius grinned. 'We'll see, we'll see.'

Cage rapped on the door.

'I'm ready, Deputy,' he said.

CHAPTER 6

From Dodge City, Ben Cage and John Chance set a course for Blackstone, Texas. Cage's only living relative, his uncle Rufus Bonner, was town marshal there. Secondly, Sophie Garrett lived there. Ben Cage and Sophie had a history.

As Cage and Johnny crossed the Red River into Texas, the sun was setting.

'Well pard, we're in Cudahey County,' said Johnny. 'We've got one more day's ride ahead of us.'

'I wonder if Cudahey County has a hotel in it where we can sleep indoors for a change?' said Cage.

'Sure,' Johnny replied cheerily. 'Rio Diablo is just about six or seven miles from here. We can put up there for the night.'

'I know Rio Diablo,' Cage said. 'I know we can get shot there but can we get a bath?'

'I know they got water there but getting it hot

and putting it in a tub may be somethin' else,' Johnny responded.

Cage gave his partner an impatient look and spurred his mount to a lope.

The hotel manager looked at them quizzically.

'Blackstone, huh? How long has it been since you were there?'

'Couple of years. Why do you ask?' Cage replied.

'Well, we used to think that Rio Diablo was wild,' the manager said. 'But in the last couple of years, things have gotten real bad in Blackstone.'

'Bad? I don't understand,' Cage said. 'I've only been gone two years. What happened in that length of time?'

'Salt,' the hotel manager said.

'Salt?' Cage repeated.

'They have big salt domes there under the ground. They mine salt, rock salt. Ship tons of salt all over the country,' the manager said. 'You know how the town started out as a farming community, don't you? One day some geologist shows up there and says there is a bunch of salt under the ground. He brings in some equipment and they put down a shaft. Sure enough, he found salt.'

'You mean they dig this stuff out of a mine?' Johnny asked.

'Nope, not like coal-mining. They squirt hot water down into the ground and it dissolves the salt and they pump it out and collect the salt.

Damnedest thing you ever saw. Anyway, there have been some disputes over ownership rights, mineral rights and that sort of thing. They had quite a war, year and a half ago. After enough people got killed, things calmed down. That is, calmed down relative to what they were,' he added with a grin. 'Now Rio Diablo looks like a church lawn party in comparison.'

Cage and Johnny exchanged looks.

'I think we better go take a look at my old stomping ground, hadn't we?' Cage said.

'I reckon so, partner. But it sounds like the place fell apart after you left. We'd better go fix it.'

No one took notice of them when they rode into town. As far as the citizens of Blackstone were concerned, they were just two cowhands, two more of a breed that passed through their county by the scores.

The town they had known two years previously had disappeared. There were at least a dozen more saloons on the main street and they saw three bordellos on the north edge of town. Girls, naked from the waist up, displayed their charms in the second-floor windows of the bagnios, beckoning to passersby and entreating them to dally awhile in paradise. Johnny had a high time exchanging jibes with the girls.

Cage and Johnny dismounted in front of the town marshal's office and looked around. They marveled at the changes two years and a salt mine had wrought.

They tied up their mounts and walked into the office. An old man with a grizzled gray beard and a balding head with a badge pinned to his shirt sat behind the desk, sound asleep.

Cage cleared his throat but got no response from the sleeping man. He cleared his throat again, more loudly. No response. He walked to a large door with a small barred window in it and pulled it open. The hinges' squeak got no response so he slammed the heavy door shut.

The boom of the shutting door brought the old man to his feet, wide-eyed and clutching at the pistol on his hip.

'Don't bother to draw, Uncle Rufus,' Cage said. 'We're friends.'

The marshal blinked his eyes in confusion and looked from Johnny to Cage and back again.

'Benjamin? Is that you?' he cried.

'The one and only,' Cage said.

The marshal grabbed Cage in his arms.

Cage, startled by the bear hug, looked surprised but then smiled and hugged the old man back.

'Uncle Rufus, this is my partner, John Chance,' said Cage.

'Glad to meetcha,' said Rufus, shaking Johnny's hand warmly.

Rufus told his guests to sit down. He rummaged around in a drawer and pulled out three tin cups, handing them each one. Then he produced a bottle of whiskey from his desk drawer and poured three stiff shots.

'We might's well celebrate,' he said. 'Here's to family!'

He tossed off the shot and poured himself another. Cage took a sip of his. Johnny tossed his down and gasped for air.

'Have another!' Rufus said.

'No thanks,' Johnny said, his eyes watering.

'I got about a thousand questions for you boys,' Rufus said. 'Ben, you must have heard about what happened after you left.'

'No, Uncle Rufus,' Cage said. 'I haven't heard a thing out of Blackstone since I rode out of here.'

Rufus raised his eyebrows in surprise.

'After you left, they went over Oleman's books and started looking for the money that folks had invested in his mining company. They couldn't find it. There was no equipment; there was no land acquisition, there was nothing. They sent a couple of bank examiners to Dallas and Fort Worth and they found a place that Oleman had bought and furnished with the investors' money. They found out he used to have the place full of girls and champagne and friends and hell-raising. Harvey Oleman had blown it all.'

'Everybody lost their money is what you're saying.'

'That's what I'm saying. And those were the folks

that ran you out of town. They found out that when you challenged Oleman, he was bluffing. If you hadn't killed him, someone else would have when they found out that they'd been screwed outta all that money. And you know something, Ben. Those are the ones that won't look me in the eye anymore.'

They talked till the sun was low in the sky and Rufus started running out of questions. He noticed it was dark in the office and he lit a coal-oil lantern.

'Now I've got a question,' said Cage.

'What's that?'

'What's been happening around here? We were told by someone in Rio Diablo that Blackstone has taken first place among the bad towns in Texas.'

Rufus looked unhappy.

'Let's talk about that later,' he said and quickly changed the subject. 'I'll bet you boys are hungry, ain't you?' he asked. 'And by the way, you got a place to stay?'

'No, Uncle Rufus,' Cage answered. 'I kind of figured we'd stay at that hotel down the street.'

'Oh no!' Rufus said. 'You don't want to do that. They'll rob you blind in that place. You can spend tonight with me and tomorrow we'll get you a room at the boarding-house with a lady I know. C'mon, let's go eat.'

Rufus led the two trail hands down into the next block to a place with a sign that said:

GRACE HOLLIS
EATS

They hung their hats on pegs by the door and took a table. A very large woman whom Cage remembered as Grace Hollis approached them.

'Well Rufus, land's sake alive!' she said. 'The sun has gone down and you're still sober. Special occasion?' she asked, eyeing Cage and Johnny.

'Grace, my dear,' Rufus said with a slight sneer, 'this is my nephew Ben Cage and his riding partner, Johnny Chance. They've come to town to visit with me for a while.'

Graced examined Cage closely.

'Wouldn't have picked him for one of your relatives, Rufus,' she said. 'Looks like he bathes and shaves every once in a while, and he's not too bad-looking and his friend is kinda pretty. Always figured your relatives would drag their knuckles when they walked.'

'That's funny, Grace,' Rufus said sarcastically. 'Got anything back in this roach pit of yours that's fit to eat?'

'The usual,' she answered, a shade impatiently. 'Beef stew and cornbread for two bits, ham steak and eggs for four bits, T-bone steak and potatoes for six bits.'

Rufus leaned close to Cage and, shielding his mouth with his hand, whispered: 'Get the beef stew. It's the best in the state but I don't want her

68

hearing me say that.'

'I'll have the beef stew and coffee,' said Cage.

'I'll have the same,' Johnny said.

'Three beef stews,' she said, walking away.

'Uncle Rufus,' Cage said, 'you didn't answer my question about what has been going on.'

Rufus looked down at the table, thinking. When he looked up, he was almost apologetic.

'It is a tough town,' he said softly. 'It's tough on anyone who doesn't want to go by the rules. You go by the rules, everything is fine.'

Cage was puzzled.

'You mean, Uncle Rufus, that you're the one that's tough on people if they break the law?'

Rufus smiled ruefully.

'Not me, the people that run things here. They keep me around to clean up.'

He glanced around to make certain no one could overhear and leaned across the table, dropping his voice.

'I just keep things neat and take care of the paperwork. As long as I do that to please 'em, I keep my job.'

'What do you mean?'

Rufus held up his hand to stop the questions.

'No questions. Wait till we get home, then we can talk,' he said.

That evening, they sat around the small table in Rufus's modest two-room home and talked. Rufus got out a bottle of whiskey and poured himself a drink. His two guests declined.

'Sorry you'll have to use your bedrolls tonight, fellows,' Rufus said. 'The only sleeping-accommodations I got is that cot over there. But at least you'll be in out of the weather.'

'That's all right, Uncle Rufus,' Cage said. 'We've been sleeping outdoors on the ground for the better part of two months. Having a roof over our heads is the lap of luxury. And besides, our horses are in a nice shed and have plenty of oats, so they're happy too.'

'Uncle Rufus,' Johnny said, 'you were going to tell us about your job.'

Rufus poured himself another drink and gazed into the glass.

'I'm not proud of what's gone on but I'll tell you and let you decide. As you know, there were three ways to make a living here before the salt-mine opened: farming, ranching and running a store. The railroad came in here because of the salt-mine, and it turned out good for everybody. Some folks built a slaughterhouse a coupla miles outside of town. The local ranchers are saving a lot of stock for the local market and three hog farms have got started.

'Westbound people headin' to El Paso and points west come through here and stop. Then we get a lot of people and cattle moving north up to Kansas. When the salt-mine people came in – it's called Colosimo Mining, by the way – they set out to acquire certain land, mineral rights and water rights. That's when the trouble started. I don't pretend to understand all of it, but a lot of folks they tried to deal with felt like the company was trying to squeeze 'em and get the rights for chicken-feed. Then too, they needed to divert water from the Trinity branch for what they needed. There was a problem with getting the right of way to run the water-pipe through some folk's property and a problem with folks downstream who didn't want the water-level to drop more than it already had. I won't go into all the details, but that's when folks started having accidents.'

Cage leaned forward. 'And the people who were dying were the ones who wouldn't accept the deal the company offered.'

'Right,' Rufus answered. 'You remember Hank Campbell, the town marshal? He got to asking questions about a couple of those accidents. One night somebody shot him in the back. A couple of the landowners went over to the county seat and talked to Sheriff Turnbull. That wasn't their first choice since the sheriff wasn't known for his honesty in the first place. Of course, he smiled in their faces and told 'em he'd be over and look into things at Blackstone. When he showed up at last, he spent most of his time laughing and drinkin' out at the mine-manager's house.

'Course the widows of the fellows that died could-n't hold out and they sold on the company's terms and moved away to be close to their families. Others sold out because they were scared. Things eventually got settled down. They made me the marshal and if I didn't ask too many questions, nobody bothered me. Every once in a while, I'd get called when somebody got hisself shot. The witnesses would say it was self-defence, so that's the way I'd put it in the record. I fooled myself into thinking that everything was on the up and up. Of course, there were a few of those "self-defense" cases where the dead man had been shot in the back. By the time I'd figured it all out, it was too late for me to get out. I'm too old to go somewhere else and when I retire from this job, I get a little pension. So I can't afford to rock the boat.'

Rufus got up and paced the room while Cage and Johnny sat in silence.

'The truth is I feel like I sold my soul. But I'm too old and too damned scared to do anything about it.'

The old man sat back down wearily, slumping into his chair.

'In fact,' he went on, 'the whole damned town has turned out that way. Everybody is scared to do anything. As long as we toe the company line, we'll be in the chips. Business is good and no one wants to do anything to hurt that.'

There was silence.

'Damn!' Johnny said, amazed. 'What a mess!'

'You're right,' Cage said. 'It's a mess and a big one but I can't see what anyone can do about it. I reckon all the county records are on the up and up, the company has what it wants. Shouldn't be too much more going on.'

Rufus looked up.

'There wouldn't be much goin' on if it weren't for Billy Benteen,' Rufus offered.

'Who is Billy Benteen?' Cage asked.

'He's the company enforcer, does all the dirty work.'

'Pretty tough fellow?' Cage asked.

'God knows how many men he's killed,' Rufus answered, shaking his head. 'He's a nasty son of a bitch, treats everyone in town like dirt 'cept for those in tight with the mine-manager.'

'Who is the mine-manager?' Johnny asked.

'Fellow by the name of Abe Clinton, from somewhere up north. Cold fish son of a bitch.'

'Cold fish?' Johnny asked, chuckling.

'Never changes expression as far as I can tell, whether he's ordering a drink or having somebody shot. I don't think there's an ounce of sorrow or joy in his whole body. Never heard of him bein' with a woman, never even saw him laugh.'

'Doesn't sound like much fun to me.' Johnny sniggered. 'Why be a big shot if you can't run the girls?'

'So we keep our eyes peeled for Billy Benteen,' Cage stated. 'What does he look like?'

Rufus looked up at the ceiling, thinking.

'You know how mamas scare their kids into bein'

good by tellin' 'em the boogie man will get 'em?'

'Yeh,' Johnny answered.

'In Blackstone,' Rufus said, 'They tell 'em that Billy Benteen will get 'em. What does he look like? I calculate that when he was born his mama took one look and throwed him away. Ugly son of a bitch! 'Bout six feet tall. Skinny. Bug-eyed. Teeth stick out too, right in front. Walks around with his mouth open like he don't have good sense. When he shuts his mouth and tries to close his lips over those teeth, I swear to God, his mouth looks like a horse's ass.'

'Wow, that must be one bad-looking *hombre!*' Cage exclaimed. 'We shouldn't have any trouble recognizing him.'

The two young men chuckled.

Rufus smiled and held up his index finger.

'But don't sell him short. He's a fast son of a bitch with his gun. And if he don't want to try to outdraw you, he'll shoot you in the back first chance he has. He's got a sidekick too, a sniveling little bastard that keeps his nose up Benteen's ass. His name is Luther. When he's around, watch out for your whiskey and your wallet.'

'Where did this Benteen come from?' Cage asked.

Rufus frowned, trying to remember.

'Came from somewhere over on the other side of the county. I understand he didn't have any folks, stayed with first one family, then another. Grew up mean. He had no people who would claim him; half-starved most of the time, got kicked around and worked at odd jobs. Disappeared for a while then showed up again carrying a pistol and working for Colosimo. Personally I think he's making up for all that time he was on the bottom.'

He stood up and took down his suspenders.

' 'Bout time for some shut-eye, boys,' he said, yawning. 'Sweet dreams.'

Cage rolled out his bedroll.

'Why do I have a feeling I'm going to dream about Billy Benteen tonight?' he asked no one in particular.

CHAPTER 7

The next day, while Johnny Chance looked around the town with Uncle Rufus, Cage decided to check on Sophie Garrett. He had no idea of whether she was married, still single or perhaps betrothed to someone. Cage made a quick mental inventory of the men in Blackstone and came up with few who were worthy of Sophie Garrett.

The last time he had seen Sophie, she and her brother, Lee, were running the general store on the main street a block down from the marshal's office. He walked to the store and went in. As he opened the door, a little bell tinkled overhead. He stopped and looked around the interior, hoping to see Lee Garrett. Lee was not in sight nor were there any customers.

From behind, he heard a feminine voice.

'May I help you find something?'

Cage turned and started to answer. It was Sophie!

It was an older, more mature and, it seemed to

Cage, a more beautiful Sophie. Her hair was still blond, only slightly darker than when he left. Her blue eyes sparkled from a flawless face that seemed to glow and light up her surroundings. She had strong cheekbones and a shapely and symmetrical nose that blended with her face to perfection. She was of medium height, standing five feet five. She wore a white Gibson-girl blouse topped by a high collar and a black tie with a black calico skirt covering her ankles. The outfit accentuated her incredibly slender waist and her generous bosom. He swiftly concluded that her smile alone was worth the ride to Blackstone.

When she saw Cage's face, the smile disappeared.

'Ben Cage,' she said, her voice flat, without inflection.

'Sophie?' he whispered.

'What brings you back to Blackstone?' she asked, airily.

'You're not glad to see me?'

'Why? Should I be?'

'One of the reasons I came back here was to see you, Sophie.'

'It's a little late to be worrying about me isn't it, Ben Cage?'

'I've been worrying about you for two years, Sophie.'

'But you left.'

'Yes, I left, for some damned good reasons. I just wish you had left with me.'

Sophie's hands were trembling and she put them behind her back.

'I was afraid.'

'Afraid? Afraid of me?'

'You know how I feel about violence, Ben; because of the way my father died. When you killed Harvey Oleman, all of a sudden I didn't know you. I saw your face after you killed him. What I saw frightened me.'

'That's in the past,' Cage said. 'You above all people should have known me by then. Anyway, I came over here because I wanted to see you and find out what has happened since I left.'

'A lot has happened since you left, Ben,' she said in a voice devoid of emotion. 'I got married.'

Cage's face fell and his shoulders slumped.

She smirked at his expression.

'You didn't expect me to wait for someone who walked out and didn't even write a letter for two years, did you?' she asked sharply.

'No, of course not,' Cage said resignedly. 'Who did you marry?'

'Jim Harris,' she replied.

'Jim Harris. Yeah, I know him,' he said without enthusiasm. 'Good man. I'm sure you're happy.'

'Not any more,' she said without emotion. 'We were married for only a year when Billy Benteen killed him.'

Cage stared at her in stunned silence. She struggled to keep her composure but he saw a tremor in her lower lip.

'My God!' he exclaimed. 'Oh Sophie, I'm so sorry. Oh Lord, what can I say?'

'There's nothing anyone can say,' she answered. 'Nothing will bring him back. And you're right; he was a good man. You left and he wanted me and then he died.'

Tears started flowing down her cheeks and she wiped at them with the backs of her hands.

He reached out to her and she collapsed against his chest, racked by deep sobs. He held her, too overwhelmed with surprise and guilt to speak.

A voice came from the back of the store:

'Sophie, are you all right?'

The speaker came around a corner and saw them. It was Lee, Sophie's brother. He stopped when he recognized Cage. He stood watching Sophie for a moment with sadness in his eyes. He nodded to Cage and disappeared.

The sobs slowed and eventually stopped. Sophie pushed back from his embrace and glanced at him.

'I can't do this,' she said. 'I have work to do.'

She turned to go.

'Lee is here somewhere. You'll want to speak to him.'

She disappeared into the back of the store.

Cage walked up an aisle and saw Lee. He walked up and offered his hand. Lee shook it warmly.

'It's good to see you, Ben,' he said, smiling. 'I was afraid you'd never come back here.'

'I came back to make a decision, Lee,' Cage said. 'I have an attractive offer to work on a ranch as a foreman, trail boss or what have you. But I wanted to make sure first. I wanted to see Sophie and try to make things right with her.'

'She was awfully unhappy when you left, Ben. But she took up with Jim Harris and seemed to be happy again. They married and I thought she was set for life. Then Jim got into it with the Colosimo Company. Sophie told you about Jim?'

'Yes,' Cage said. 'What happened?'

Lee sat down on a barrel.

'Jim was in the building business. He was good at it and he hired some carpenters from places around here. He was doing pretty good, had some contracts with the salt company. He started getting edgy when some of the folks the company was dealing with had strange accidents. When Billy Benteen killed two men in one week and pleaded "self-defense" and the so-called witnesses backed him up, it got to be too much for Jim. He went to see Clinton and told him about his suspicions. Clinton listened to him and said that those were serious charges and he'd look into it right away. Two days later he was dead. The story was that he got into a gunfight with Billy Benteen out at one of his building sites.'

Cage frowned.

'Jim Harris in a gunfight? I don't remember him ever carrying a gun.'

'He didn't,' Lee answered. 'He didn't even own

one. But Benteen's witnesses said Jim was armed. They had an old Colt rimfire .44 that he was supposed to have been carrying.'

'Self-defense?' Cage asked.

'Sure,' Lee answered with a grim smile. 'It almost killed Sophie. I've never seen her that way. I began to think she wasn't going to recover. But she's sticking it out like the rest of us. We swallow our pride and go about our business. Times are good so no one complains. But it's Abe Clinton who calls the shots here in Blackstone.'

'I heard the same thing from someone else,' Cage said.

Sophie came out of the back room. She had washed her face and only a little redness remained around her eyes.

'You fellows talking about old times?' she asked.

'No, as a matter of fact,' Lee said. 'We were talking about Ben taking you to lunch down at Grace Hollis's place, weren't we, Ben.'

Sophie looked bewildered.

'Well, I don't . . . I don't want to leave you. . . .'

'Don't worry about me,' Lee said. 'It's a slow day. Besides, you and Ben have some talking to do. Go on!'

Sophie did not look pleased at the position her brother had put her in. They went out the front door and turned toward the next block. When they met some people on the boardwalk, Sophie greeted them cheerily. Suddenly, she took Cage's hand.

He reveled in her touch. He had forgotten how long it had been since he had been touched by a feminine hand with true affection.

Then Cage saw the reason she had taken his hand. Two men were walking toward them on the boardwalk. The taller of the two was incredibly ugly and he walked with his mouth open and his teeth showing. His smaller companion was rat-faced and greasy-looking.

About that time the two men met them and the tall one looked at Sophie, pushed out his ugly lips and made smacking noises. His companion stuck out his tongue and made slurping noises.

Ben stopped.

'What the . . .' he said.

'Don't, Ben,' Sophie said quickly.

'I'm not going to let that goat-herder act that way toward a lady!' Ben almost shouted.

'It's all right, Ben. Don't pay any attention. He's dangerous!' Sophie said, her voice lowered. 'Come on.'

The two men had stopped on the boardwalk and were looking back at them. The taller one smiled nastily.

'Ben, come on!' Sophie almost shouted. 'He'll kill you. You're not even wearing a gun.'

She tugged at his arm and Cage started moving, glancing back at the offender.

'Why do I have to let him get away with that?' Cage demanded.

'That was Billy Benteen,' she said. 'Don't mess with him.'

Cage stopped and turned. The two men had continued on their way.

'That's what I thought,' he muttered. 'Yet another reason.'

'What do you mean, "another reason"?' Sophie asked.

'Never mind,' Cage said, forcing himself to calm down. 'Never mind.'

Cage and Sophie managed to get through their meal at Grace Hollis's place speaking in civilized tones. The sharp edge had left Sophie's voice as they discussed mutual friends and long-ago events.

At last Sophie said: 'About a month after you left, everybody found out you were right.'

'That's what I understand.'

'The people who spoke the loudest against you shut up and wouldn't say anything, no apologies, no nothing. When they saw your Uncle Rufus in the street, they wouldn't even look him in the eye.'

Cage nodded.

'I wanted you to come back but no one knew where you were,' Sophie said softly. 'After six months I figured, everyone figured, you were gone for good. That's why, when Jim Harris came around and asked me out, I went.'

'Sophie,' Cage said, reaching across the table and putting his hand on hers, 'you don't have to explain anything to me. Your first responsibility was, and still is, yourself.'

'You don't have any resentment?'

'Am I envious of Jim Harris because you were his wife and you loved him and let him make love to you? Yes, I am. And no matter what happens from here on out, I always will be. Do I resent it? No. I can't resent people trying to be happy. God knows it's hard enough in this world to be happy.'

Sophie put her other hand on top of Cage's.

Cage and Johnny walked through the swing-doors of the Black Stallion saloon at three o'clock in the afternoon and leaned against the bar. They had taken the precaution of wearing their guns.

There were few tipplers in the bar. One was asleep at a back table and two more were engaged in a game of dominoes.

'What'll you have?' the bartender asked.

'I'll have a beer,' Cage said.

'Let me have a drink of your finest whiskey,' Johnny said, smiling.

The bartender took his time drawing Cage's beer and set it in front of him. Then he set a shot-glass in front of Johnny and poured it full from a bottle that he selected from a large number behind the bar.

Johnny tossed down the whiskey, gasped and grimaced.

When he regained his voice, he said, 'Hoo, boy! Are you sure that is your best whiskey?'

'Must be,' the bartender said, without changing expression. 'It don't eat the varnish off the bar when you spill it.'

Johnny shook his head rapidly.

'Well in that case, give me another shot, mister . . .'

'Brewster,' the bartender said.

As Brewster poured another shot Johnny asked:

'Mr Brewster, where can a man get into a game of poker around here?'

'Hang around a few hours and you can get a game back there at the round table,' Brewster replied, tilting his head toward the back of the room.

'Who runs it?' Johnny asked.

'Crawdad Jones runs the game usually.'

'Crawdad?' Johnny asked. 'How will I know him?'

'He's got only a forefinger and a thumb on his left hand. Got one of his fingers chawed off in a fight, got the other two shot off. His hand looks like a crawdad* claw. You can't miss him.'

Johnny turned to Cage.

'What do you say we come down this evening and get in the game, partner?' he asked enthusiastically.

'What do you mean, "we", Chance?' asked Cage. 'Don't you mean you'll get in the game and I'll watch your back?'

'Well, sure,' Johnny said. 'But we always make a good team.'

* Crayfish.

Cage finished his beer and they walked back to the marshal's office. Uncle Rufus was there and looked up smiling when they entered.

'I got you a room at Mrs Biffle's house,' he announced proudly. 'Got a regular bed in it, a wardrobe and a wash-stand. She's got a big wash-tub you can use for taking a bath if you're so inclined. It'll cost you four bits a night each, payable in advance and breakfast is throwed in. I told her you'd probably stay a week anyway. And she's got a shed for your horses.'

'Is this Mrs Biffle a clean and orderly lady, Uncle Rufus? I don't want to get waked up in the night by a big roach crawlin' across my face.'

'The cleanest there is,' Rufus said.

They went to Rufus's shack and picked up their gear. They moved it into the boarding-house under Mrs Biffle's watchful eye.

Mrs Biffle was tall and thin with thin lips to match and with graying black hair pulled on top of her head in a tight bun. After they had stowed their gear, she explained the rules.

'There will be no use of alcohol or tobacco of any kind on the premises, gentlemen,' she said, turning a suspicious eye on Johnny. 'Rent is payable a week in advance. After nine o'clock, there will be no loud talk and no singing. At no time will bringing female friends into the house be tolerated. The privy is right out in back and it is to be kept neat and clean. There is a wash-tub available for bathing; you heat your own water in the pot out back. You will empty your own chamber-pot. Is that understood?'

'Yes ma'am,' the boys answered in unison.

'Breakfast is at seven every morning,' she went on. 'If you're not at the table before a quarter of eight, you do without.'

'Yes'm,' they replied.

After escaping from Mrs Biffle, the boys returned to town and checked in with Uncle Rufus. After telling him that the room arrangements were to their satisfaction, they drifted back toward the Black Stallion by way of the general store. As they walked by the store, Cage saw Sophie waiting on a female customer. They were examining a bolt of cloth. Sophie glanced up and smiled a quick smile, then returned her attention to her customer.

She was going to a church fellowship meeting that evening so Cage had made arrangements to call on her at home the next night.

Cage and Johnny took a table in the saloon and both ordered beer. They sipped on their beer and watched the crowd slowly build as the evening wore on. After some time a crusty-looking character in a high-crowned hat and wearing shapeless woolen trousers with suspenders over an undershirt walked in and was greeted by a half-dozen of the locals. His left hand was a mutilated mess but the forefinger and thumb seemed to be fully functional. He sat down at the big round table in the back of the room and started to shuffle a deck of cards.

Johnny winked at Cage and got up. He strolled casually to the card-table. Crawdad looked up and regarded him suspiciously.

'Who the hell are you,' he barked.

'Johnny Chance,' came the answer. 'I'm looking for a straight poker game.'

'Johnny Chance?' Crawdad said. 'Sounds like a professional card-sharp name to me.'

'Nope,' Johnny said. 'Just a trail hand. I'm in town visiting my friend's uncle, Rufus Bonner.'

Crawdad threw back his head and guffawed.

'Rufus Bonner! Jesus! Anybody that would claim knowing that old bastard must be honest. Most folks would lie about it. Sit down, kid.'

Johnny slid into a chair and removed his hat.

The five-card draw game was well into its third hour and Johnny was winning, along with a newcomer to town called Brazos Bob Dugan. There had been six people in the game but one had gone broke and pulled out. Impressed with the skill of the players, no one among the spectators offered to sit in.

While he played, Johnny sipped sarsaparilla and made certain that the barmaid kept the other players' glasses full of whiskey. Though Johnny was having a high time, Cage was getting bored. He thought about going down the street to another place but decided against it. He knew Johnny was good at the game and played the odds, rarely taking a chance. But sometimes he was too good and it wasn't unknown for a sore loser to accuse him of cheating. That was when Cage's presence was needed.

Cage calculated that the game would end soon with Johnny and Brazos Bob winning. Crawdad was breaking even and Cage could tell by his gestures of impatience that the old card-player was tiring of the day's game. The two other players, called Sid and Morgan, had been losing steadily and their cash was dwindling fast.

It was Crawdad's deal and the action picked up. Johnny opened with a five-dollar bet. Brazos Bob called and raised the bet by five dollars. Crawdad matched the bet and raised it another five. Sid folded. Johnny and Morgan called. Crawdad called for cards and Johnny drew one. Brazos Bob and Crawdad each drew two. Morgan drew one.

The last raiser, Crawdad, chuckled and bet five. Johnny called and raised another five. Brazos called and Morgan called. They were about to lay down their hands when someone leaned over the table and grabbed the pot.

'You boys know I'm supposed to be cut in on all the poker games around here.' he said. 'This ought to make it square.'

Everyone had been intent on the game and no one but Cage had noticed Billy Benteen walking in and moseying up to the table. Cage was already moving when Benteen grabbed the poker pot. He slowly eased to a position behind the gunman while keeping his eyes on the slimy little rat-faced man who had walked in with him.

Benteen smiled. 'Crawdad,' he said, 'you are goin' to screw up one too many times and that's goin' to be the end of you.'

Crawdad looked terrified and started to sputter an explanation. The other players sat still and stared at Benteen with undisguised hatred.

Johnny stood up. 'Everybody hold on to his hand,' he said. He turned to Benteen and asked: 'Who the hell are you to grab that pot?'

Benteen looked surprised.

'Who am I?' he said, grinning. 'Someone tell him who I am.'

'They don't need to tell me your name, Benteen,' said Johnny, sneering. 'Seeing as how you're ugly as a trough full of hog-guts it's no trouble picking you out. My question is where in hell do you get off grabbin' that damned pot?'

Benteen's mouth fell open and he took a step back. The spectators turned over chairs in their rush to get from behind Johnny.

'You stupid ass,' said Benteen. He started to draw. Cage grabbed his gun arm and simultaneously clubbed the gunman with the butt of his own six-shooter. Benteen crumpled to the floor.

Benteen's companion gasped.

'You can't do that!' he shrieked.

Cage looked at him.

'I'll do any damn thing I get ready to do, worm,' he said.

The man paled and stepped back.

Cage leaned over Benteen and removed the gunman's single-action Colt .45 from its holster. He rotated the cylinder and ejected each of the six cartridges on to the floor. Then he frisked the inert body and came up with a hunting-knife and a derringer two-shot .32. He unloaded the derringer and laid the knife on the floor. He put his foot on the blade and pulled up on the hilt. The blade snapped neatly and Cage dropped the hilt to the floor. The crowd watched in slack-jawed amazement.

Someone in the crowd spoke.

'You are either the dumbest damned cowboy in this town or you're the meanest son of a bitch that ever walked.'

'I guarantee you, folks, I'm neither one,' Cage said.

Then Johnny sat down again and spoke.

'Let's finish the hand, fellows,' he said, casually.

The other players slowly recovered their senses and picked up their hands.

'What have you got?' Johnny said, laying down a full house, kings high. With trembling hands, Crawdad laid down three queens. Morgan laid down a full house, eights high and Brazos Bob Dugan laid down four deuces.

There was a loud exclamation from the crowd.

Crawdad picked up what he had left.

'That's enough for me fellows,' he said, and hastily departed.

The others agreed it was time to call it a night. Dugan went over to where Benteen lay and picked up his pot.

'Damn, it's been nice meeting you fellows,' he said. 'I owe you a favor.'

'I'll remember that,' Cage said, extending his hand.

Dugan shook Cage's hand and took his leave, tipping his hat.

Johnny and Cage walked outside and took a breath of clean air.

As they walked out, Luther, Benteen's companion, rushed to his side and tried to rouse him.

'I almost left and went down the street,' Cage said. 'It's a damned good thing I didn't.'

Johnny looked at him and grinned.

'Hell, you don't think I woulda opened my mouth if I hadn't seen you behind him? I may be kind of nuts but I ain't that crazy.' He sniggered, then laughed out loud. 'He coulda had that pot with my blessings.'

'Well, we got to meet Benteen and Luther,' Cage said.

'Luther looks a lot like a greasy rat, don't he?' Johnny opined.

'I think you summed it up,' Ben agreed.

'Ben,' Johnny said. 'We just made an enemy of

the meanest son of a bitch in this town.'

'You said a mouthful there,' said Cage. 'Let's go home and try Mrs Biffle's bed.'

CHAPTER 8

The next morning, at breakfast, Cage and Johnny found that the news of their confrontation with the town bully had already spread. One of the diners was excited about sitting at the table with the trail hand who had put Billy Benteen down.

'Did you know who it were that you cold-cocked?' he asked Cage, wide-eyed.

Cage nodded.

'You can't miss him,' he said. 'That face could scare a hungry dog out of town.'

The tableful of boarders whooped and laughed.

'Speakin' of bein' scart out of town,' another one said, 'I understand Old Crawdad has done left. He sure as heck din't want to be around when Benteen woke up.'

'What you goin' to do when Benteen comes after you?' asked a third.

Cage looked serious.

'Well,' he said, 'that depends on whether he

94

wants a fair fight, or decides to do some back-shooting. I suppose we'll have to deal with whatever comes along.'

'Benteen is the quickest draw in the county from what I hear,' the third boarder said. 'Are you pretty fast, mister?'

Cage looked at the questioner, but before he could answer, Johnny broke in.

'The fastest between Texas and Dodge City,' he said, smiling. 'He can shoot you, reload and have his .44 back in the holster before you hit the ground.'

The boarders whooped again.

'In Dodge City,' Johnny went on, before the laughter died, 'they won't let you carry a gun in town. Old Ben here caught a murderer who was armed, took his gun away from him and whipped him with his bare hands.'

'That's enough, Johnny,' Cage admonished gently. 'Before we know it, you'll have me riding a cyclone and whipping it with a rattlesnake like Pecos Bill.'

The boarders chuckled, but one of them, an older man dressed in black, spoke seriously. 'My friend, don't sell Benteen short. He's fast and he'll try to fake you into going for your gun first. Two weeks ago I saw him kill a man downtown. The two of 'em squared off and Benteen jerked his left arm like he was going for a gun on his left side. Of course he doesn't wear one on his left side. The other fellow was so nervous that when Benteen made that little move, he went for his gun first. But Benteen beat him to the draw and killed him in the middle of the street with a single shot. I'd be careful if I were you.'

'That's good advice, sir. I'm much obliged to you,' Cage said.

'What kind of work do you do?' Johnny asked.

'I suppose you can say I'm a troubleshooter,' the man answered. 'By the way, did you notice that Benteen carries a single-action Colt .45?'

'Yes, I did,' Cage replied.

'I see you carry a double-action .44. Wise choice. That gives you a tenth of a second advantage.'

'Not much margin for error there,' Cage stated.

'Not much,' the older man said, smiling. 'Good day, gentlemen and good luck.'

'That's a strange bird,' said Johnny. 'You ready to go downtown?'

'Let's ride,' answered Cage.

When Cage and Johnny rode up, there was a crowd in the street in front of the marshal's office. Someone was on the ground and the curious were crowding around.

The pair dismounted and walked over to the crowd. 'Here's his nephew,' they heard someone say.

Hearing that, Cage pushed his way through the bystanders. Rufus Bonner lay in the street, bleeding.

'Uncle Rufus!' Cage cried. He fell to his knees

beside the mortally wounded man.

Blood bubbled from a massive wound in the middle of the old man's chest. He started coughing and Cage held up his head. Blood trickled from the side of his mouth.

Rufus opened his eyes and focused on Cage's face.

'Ben,' he said and a faint smile touched his lips.

'Who did this, Uncle Rufus?' Cage asked, softly.

'Benteen,' came the barely audible answer.

'Why?' Cage cried.

The old man seemed to gather his strength to answer.

'Wanted to know where you were.' Smiling, the old man added: 'I told him to go to hell.'

The old man coughed and more blood came out of his mouth. He spoke again, gurgling.

'Turned my back . . . on him . . . and walked away . . . he's nothing.'

A shudder racked Rufus's frame and his breath passed from his body in a long sigh. His eyes remained open, so Cage closed them and continued kneeling there in the street, holding his uncle's head.

'Benteen shot him in the back,' someone in the crowd said.

'That's right,' another bystander said. 'I saw the whole thing.'

'Benteen must be completely crazy, shooting a law officer in the back,' another voice said.

Cage gently laid Rufus's head down and rose to his feet.

'Is there an undertaker in this town?' he asked.

'Grundy the barber is an undertaker on the side,' someone said.

Cage handed a small boy a coin.

'Go get Mr Grundy,' he said.

'Yessir,' answered the boy and scampered away.

'Anybody see where Benteen went?' Cage asked the crowd.

'I saw him and his suck-ass friend riding out of town, heading south,' said a man at the edge of the crowd.

Cage turned and addressed the bystanders in a loud voice.

'Those of you who saw what happened, are you willing to testify in a court of law about what you saw?' he asked.

There was no answer. Cage asked his question again. The bystanders averted their eyes and started drifting away.

'What's the matter? I'm going after the sheriff. Won't anyone tell him what he saw? Are you afraid?'

'You damned right, they're afraid,' came a voice.

It was Brewster, the bartender from the Black Stallion.

'They know the sheriff works for the same people that pay Benteen,' he said. 'Their lives wouldn't be worth a plugged nickel if they swore to anything.'

'You're telling me that the law won't do anything

about this – a law officer getting shot in the back?' Cage asked.

'That's what I'm telling you,' the bartender said. 'If you want justice, you'll have to get it with that pistol you're carrying, mister. We've seen that murdering bastard get away with too much for us to count on the law.'

Brewster looked at Rufus's body, shook his head and walked back toward his saloon.

'He's right, you know,' someone in back of Cage said.

Cage turned. It was Dick Cartwright, mayor of Blackstone.

'No one here has what it takes to face Benteen,' the mayor went on. 'Everyone has given up.'

Cage, Johnny and Cartwright stood there together until Grundy arrived with his wagon. They helped Grundy load the body on the bed of the wagon, then they went into the marshal's office.

Cage sat at his uncle's desk and closed his eyes.

'It's my fault,' he said. 'I slugged Benteen when I should have killed him. I made a mistake and Uncle Rufus paid for it.'

'It's not your fault, Ben,' Johnny said. 'Benteen must be stark staring crazy to shoot a harmless old man in the back for a reason like that. You had no way of knowing he'd take it out on Rufus.'

Cage paused and looked around the office.

'Let's get my uncle buried and then take care of Benteen. If anyone gives us any shit, we'll get the hell out of here again.'

Before Johnny could speak, there was a voice from the doorway. It was Sophie.

'Running out again, Mr Cage?' she asked.

'Sophie,' Cage said, getting to his feet.

'I had hoped,' she went on, 'that maybe you and your friend might make a difference in this town.'

'It's not that,' Cage said. 'I'm going to kill Benteen. After that I figure the people who pay his salary are going to bring in someone just as nasty, and we'll have to kill him and so on. If I don't get any backing from these lily-livered sons of bitches around here, there will be no point to it.'

'You make a good point, Ben old man,' Johnny said.

Johnny and Cage rummaged through Rufus's shack and found what appeared to be his Sunday-go-to-meeting clothes and took them to Grundy. Grundy trimmed Rufus's hair and shaved him and he looked more presentable in death than most people had seen him in life.

Cage was happy to see that over a dozen folks turned out for Rufus's graveside service. Sophie and Lee Garrett were there. Mrs Biffle came and a bunch of folks whom Johnny had not met, and also Dick Cartwright, the mayor. Brazos Bob Dugan was there too. They all expressed their sorrow at Rufus's passing.

After the final amen, the mourners drifted away.

Johnny and Cage waited until the grave was filled. Cage paid the gravedigger.

'Ben, do you think Uncle Rufus and your mama are together now, talking?' Johnny asked, as they walked away.

'If what we have been told is true, they must be,' replied Cage.

Johnny looked up at the sky. 'Maybe they're talking about when they were kids out on the farm and riding their old mule,' he said. 'It makes me feel better thinking that they are, Ben.'

'Then there's nothing wrong with believing it, then,' Cage said.

There was a silence between the two men for a long moment.

'What now?' Johnny asked.

'We find Billy Benteen and kill him.'

'Now that's what I call a straight answer,' Johnny said.

CHAPTER 9

Cage and Johnny rode back to the marshal's office and went inside.

'Let's see what we have to work with,' Cage said.

They opened the gun cabinet and found an old Henry .44 rimfire lever-action rifle and a Model 1873 Winchester .38-40 carbine. In the back of a desk drawer, Cage found a .41 short four-shot pistol with a one-and-a-half-inch barrel. It was a Colt Cloverleaf, small enough for a gentleman to carry in an inside coat pocket or for a lawman to carry in a boot.

In another drawer they found ammunition for the three weapons.

While they examined the weapons, there was a knock on the door. They put the guns out of sight.

'Come in,' said Cage.

The door opened slowly and a ferret-like nose poked around the edge.

'I'm not armed,' came a voice.

Cage and Johnny exchanged puzzled glances.

'Who the hell is it?' Cage asked.

'I got a message from Billy Benteen,' the voice said.

'Come on in and let's have it,' Cage said.

The door opened further and Luther crept in.

'Well?' Cage said.

Luther drew himself up to his full unimpressive height and cleared his throat nervously.

'Billy Benteen is calling you out, Benjamin Cage,' he said. 'He will meet you at six thirty in the morning in the street right out in front here. Billy said you will have a chance to get even with him for killing your uncle and he will have the chance to get even with you for that cowardly lick you give him in the back of his head.'

Luther paused to clear his throat once again.

'He said if you are afraid to meet him, you can go ahead and leave town and he'll let you go on living,' the little man said. He paused. 'I'm s'posed to take your answer back to Billy.'

Again, Cage and Johnny exchanged glances.

Cage got up from behind the desk.

'Tell Billy Benteen that I will be out in the street at six thirty in the morning. And Luther, tell him I hope he has made his funeral arrangements. Otherwise, we'll wrap his carcass in a dirty bed-sheet from the whorehouse down the street and stuff him in a prairie-dog hole.'

Luther smirked.

'I'll tell him. Goodbye Mr Cage.'

Luther mounted his horse and rode south out of town.

Cage and Johnny walked outside and watched him ride away.

'Where do you reckon our friend Luther will be when Mr Benteen is in the street?' asked Cage.

Johnny looked around.

'I'd say he'll be hidden inside that livery stable down there, or maybe on the roof,' he said. 'Then again, he might just crawl up in the steeple at that old church over there; good place to have a view of the whole street.'

'Think you can find our friend Brazos Bob?' Cage asked.

'I reckon I can,' Johnny answered. 'You going to call that favor?'

'Yep.'

The next morning, Cage and Johnny rose early. Neither had slept well during the night and by five o'clock both were getting dressed.

'We're going to miss that sausage and biscuits and gravy this morning, Ben,' Johnny said.

'You really feel like eating?' Cage asked.

Johnny thought for a moment, frowning.

'No, I reckon not,' he said. Then he brightened and added: 'But after it's all over, we can go over to Grace's place and get ham steaks and eggs, can't we.'

'I'm planning on it,' Cage said.

They rode into town in the predawn darkness and tied up their mounts in back of the marshal's office rather than on the street. Neither wanted to risk exposing a good horse to gunfire unnecessarily. They went into the office and lit a lantern, then made coffee on the old stove.

Johnny opened the shutter on a front window and peered out at the street. He saw people moving about.

'I think the word has got out,' he said. 'Folks are already lining up for the best seats.'

There was a rap on the back door.

'That's Brazos Bob Dugan and his friend,' Cage said. 'Let him in.'

Dugan and a tall man, about six-feet four, walked in. Dugan was grinning.

'You were right, Ben,' he said. 'They came in about four this morning, Benteen and Luther. They put their mounts in the livery stable and Luther walked over to the church house carrying what looked to me like a rifle.'

'I thought so,' Cage said. Then to Johnny, he said, 'Looks like you and that old Sharps have a job to do.'

Johnny started loading the Sharps.

'Who's your friend, Dugan?' Cage asked.

'This is Raft Townsend.' Dugan made the introduction. 'Raft, this is Ben Cage and Johnny Chance.'

They shook hands while Dugan explained.

'Raft is one of the best men in a brawl or a shooting-match you could ask for. He got back in town this week and I asked him to spy on Benteen and Luther with me.'

'Good!' Cage said. 'I may need some men I can deputize. Why the name Raft? I haven't heard that one before.'

Townsend grinned. 'My big brother started calling me Rafters cause I growed so fast when I turned twelve, he said I hit my head on the rafters and that's why I was so dumb. He kept that up until I got biggr'n him and started whuppin' him. But by that time everybody was callin' me that and it got shortened to Raft and it just kind of stuck.'

'Glad to have you with us, Raft,' Cage said.

Johnny finished loading the Sharps.

'See you in a little while. I'm going up on the roof next door,' he said.

He went out the back door into the dawn.

Cage glanced at the clock. It indicated the time as six minutes past six.

Dugan and Townsend helped themselves to the coffee.

'Whooee!' Dugan gasped. 'This coffee would make a buffalo dance a jig!'

'I figured we needed to be awake for this morning's work,' Cage said.

Dugan looked into his cup.

'This will do it, all right.'

Cage pulled his .44 and checked it. All six chambers were filled. The cylinder and trigger actions were smooth. He took the Cloverleaf from the desk, checked the four cylinders and put the pistol in his right boot. He glanced at the clock again.

Dugan finished his coffee and motioned to Townsend.

'We'll be outside,' he said to Cage.

'OK,' Cage answered.

He glanced at the clock again. The pendulum swung to and fro, urging the minute-hand along an almost imperceptible distance with each click.

Cage conjured up the vision of Billy Benteen making kissing noises at Sophie. He smiled grimly as he thought that that one thing alone was enough reason for Benteen to die. Rufus was another reason and Jim Harris was yet another. Cage looked at the clock again and stood up. He opened the door and looked to his left toward the livery stable.

Benteen walked out of the stable. Cage walked out of the marshal's office and stepped into the street. He turned to his left, aware of people moving about and faces peering from windows along the street. He didn't look back. He knew that Johnny was on the roof of the building behind him. He reached the middle of the street and stopped.

Benteen walked slowly toward him and stopped. He stopped too far away for an accurate shot with a handgun. Of course, he didn't want to give Cage the advantage of being close. Benteen didn't have to be close because the rifle in the hands of his confederate would reach far enough.

'You must be a pretty good shot, Benteen,' he called out. 'That's quite a distance for a handgun.'

'It's close enough.' Benteen said, his voice unusually high.

'I think we should get a little closer,' Cage said, and started walking.

At that moment, a shot rang out behind Cage. Benteen's whole body jerked. The sound of a church bell rang out before the echo of the shot died. There was a scream, another shot from somewhere far off, a staccato clatter from the church bell, then silence.

'Sounds like somebody has bats in his belfry,' Cage said without breaking stride.

Benteen took a step back then stopped, his face drawn by fear. His left armed jerked downward. Cage did not react. Benteen went for his six-gun with his right hand. He had it out of the holster when Cage's shot hit him in the breastbone and knocked him two steps backward. Benteen's shot hit the ground by his feet. Thumbing back the hammer, Benteen tried to raise his weapon. Cage fired again. The slug hit Benteen on his left side, turning him half-way around. His knees buckled, the six-gun fell from his hand and he fell backward into the dirt and lay still.

Cage walked to where Benteen lay and stood looking down at him. Benteen looked up at Cage with a surprised expression on his face. He opened his mouth to say something but only a gurgle came out. His eyes rolled up, his mouth sagged open and his face relaxed in death.

Cage was barely aware of the cries and whoops from the sides of the street. Suddenly dozens of people, men, women and children were surrounding him and slapping him on the back. He could make out no words until Sophie appeared in front of him leaning over Billy Benteen's body.

'Damn you, Billy Benteen!' she cried. 'I hope you burn in hell forever!'

She turned at looked at Cage, her eyes shining with triumph.

Cage was stunned to see Sophie react that way. Sometime since her husband died, not only did she seem to have put aside her hatred of violence, she seemed to revel in it.

Dugan appeared beside him, whispered that he was going to check on Luther and trotted away.

Cage tried to acknowledge the congratulations and thanks being heaped on him. There were too many faces, too many handshakes and hugs. He realized his .44 was still in his hand and he replaced it in its holster.

Then Johnny was there with his arm around Cage's shoulders, leading him toward the Black Stallion saloon. They pushed through the crowd into the bar and Cage was pleased to see that Sophie was beside him.

Brewster was happily setting up shot-glasses on the bar and splashing whiskey into them. He stopped pouring long enough to draw a beer for Cage.

Cage took the beer thankfully. He had not noticed how dry his mouth had become out there in the street. The wetness of the beer was welcome as was the warming sensation as it hit his empty stomach.

Cage turned and looked at Sophie. She put her arms around his neck and kissed him on his lips. The crowd cheered.

She put her mouth close to his ear.

'You go on and have your celebration. I'll be at the store when you get time.'

With that, she scurried out the saloon door.

A man pushed his way through the well-wishers and faced the crowd, raising his arms and calling for quiet. It was Dick Cartwright, the mayor of Blackstone. When the crowd quieted, he put his left hand on Cage's shoulder and began to speak.

'Citizens of Blackstone, a native son has returned to deliver us from the clutches of Satan. Just when we were losing our civic pride and getting discouraged with our own shortcomings, Benjamin Cage has returned to show us the way. By his display of courage, he has unselfishly given us back our town.'

He turned to face Cage,

'Ben,' he said, 'two years ago you were right and we were wrong, but by the time we should have

110

been telling you that, you were gone. We looked for you, but you had lost yourself somewhere out there in the great land of Texas and we didn't even know where to start looking. Well, sir, I'm telling you now. On behalf of the citizens of Blackstone, you were right in doing what you did to Oleman, and we apologize for being too hasty in judging you. I have been talking to the members of the city council. And if you'll accept it, we'd like to offer you the job of town marshal.'

In his hand he held up the marshal's badge, the one that Rufus had worn.

Later that evening, Cage and Johnny sat in the Garretts' parlour, sipping coffee. Sophie was bustling about, pouring coffee and slicing pie. Lee sat in his favorite chair listening to Johnny talk.

'I didn't know which way to look, down in the street at Benteen and Ben or up at that belfry. When Ben started walking toward Benteen again, I knew somethin' was going to happen and sure enough, a head popped up in the belfry and I squeezed one off. I missed old Luther though and hit the bell. As it turned out, that was close enough. Dugan told me that he found the rifle and some blood at the bottom of the ladder that went up into the belfry. He climbed on up there and he could see where my shot hit the bell. He figures that a fragment of that big old bullet glanced off the bell and hit Luther somewhere and it scared him so bad, he fell out of the belfry and tried to grab the bell rope on the way down. That's why we heard that strange ringing noise. By the time Dugan got there, Luther was gone, so he couldn't have been hurt too bad.'

Cage managed a smile at Johnny's story. He was almost overcome with fatigue. A half-way sleepless night and the morning's events had taken their toll. He sat back on the couch and let Johnny and Lee talk while he watched Sophie.

He watched her move about the room and into the kitchen. She looked at him from time to time and her smile seemed like a caress.

When at last the exuberance and the excitement the others had felt at Benteen's passing began to fade they too realized how exhausted they were. When Cage and Johnny walked outside to their horses, Sophie walked out with them. She stood close to Cage and whispered.

'I wish you could stay,' she said.

'Where would I sleep?' Cage asked, smiling.

'We'd find a place,' she said coyly.

'It's been a long and tiring day,' he said. 'Let's don't rush things. I want you to get used to me being here.'

'Maybe you're right. But let's not take too much time. I've been missing out on some living. I want to catch up.'

Cage bent to her and kissed her lips gently. She responded warmly, eagerly.

Cage and Johnny rode back to their boarding-house through a cool and cloudless night without speaking. As they neared their destination, Cage spoke.

'I've found the place where I want to be, John. It's right here.'

Johnny answered: 'I reckon it'll do for me too.' He chuckled. 'Of course, if I had a lady as pretty and nice as Sophie nuzzling around on me, it'd be even better. In fact, it would just about be paradise.'

What neither of them knew was that a letter addressed to Benjamin Cage lay in the middle of the marshal's desk where the town's lone postman had placed it that afternoon. The return address was Elzee Laroux in Dodge City, Kansas. On the outside of the letter, the sender had scrawled 'Urgent'.

CHAPTER 10

Cage tore open the letter and read through it quickly.

'My God!' he said,

'What, Ben?' Johnny asked. 'What's happened?'

'Jarius Welch has escaped.'

Stunned, Johnny felt for a chair and sat down.

Cage read the letter aloud.

Ben and John, I wish I had better news to send you. Jarius Welch escaped from the Dodge City gaol before they could hang him. There was another prisoner named John Sharp waiting for hanging and his gang came in the middle of the night and broke him out and killed a deputy marshal. They took Welch with them. Sharp is a bank-robber and his gang robbed a bank the next day after they broke him out. I will try to cold-trail them and maybe give the law a hand in catching them cause I want to see Jarius dance at the end of a rope. Will write again when I know something.

Cage put the letter down and stare at it.

'Damn, Johnny! We were celebrating Billy Benteen dying yesterday and Jarius Welch is running around free.'

'Do you think he'll try to make good on that threat?' asked Johnny.

Cage looked at him.

'If he does, there's only you and Sophie I have to worry about and I'm guessing you can take care of yourself,' he answered.

'Depends on how many cowboys he brings with him to hold me down,' Johnny replied, smiling. 'Besides, Kansas is a long way off from Blackstone, Texas. He'd have to dodge the law for a long time to get down here.'

Cage shook his head.

'I wouldn't put anything past him, Johnny. He's mean as hell. And we don't know much about that gang he's running with or where they're heading.'

Cage rose from his chair and put on his hat.

'I'm going over to the telegraph office to send a message to Marshal Webb at Dodge City. We need to know about this John Sharp.'

Leaving Johnny to watch the office, Cage headed over to the depot. He hadn't gone far when he saw Sophie on the boardwalk outside the general store. He walked across the street and up behind her as she was unlocking the front door.

She turned and saw him.

'Come on in,' she said.

He followed her into the store and she put down her purse behind the counter where the cash drawer was. She walked up and put her arms around him, kissing him on the mouth. It was a wet, hungry kiss and she pressed her body to his. Her surprise actions moved and delighted him. He felt his excitement growing and pulled her against himself eagerly.

At last she broke the kiss and pushed back, looking into his eyes.

'I've thought about that all night,' she said. 'I'm ashamed of myself, but I thought about you and how it used to be.'

'Why are you ashamed of yourself?' he asked.

Her words came tumbling out.

'Because I was thinking about you and when we were together and Jim is lying out there in the cemetery and it was like I was being unfaithful to him but I'm really not because he's gone and can't come back and I was so lonely when you left but I found out what real loneliness was after he died.'

'I understand,' he replied. 'I've been thinking about you too. We did have some good times together, didn't we.'

'Do you think we can again, Ben?' she asked, looking up at him.

'After that kiss, I think we've got a good start on it,' he answered, smiling.

The store's front door opened and the bell tinkled. Sophie stepped back, patted her hair and smoothed imaginary wrinkles from her skirt.

'I'm on my way to the telegraph office,' he said. 'I'll see you in a while.'

She nodded happily and went to greet her customer.

Cage sent his telegram to Marshal Webb and asked about John Sharp and his gang, signing it Benjamin Cage, City Marshal, Blackstone, Texas. That afternoon, he was sitting in his office talking to Johnny when the answer arrived. The station agent sent it over by messenger.

It read:

JOHN SHARP CONVICTED KILLER VERY DANGEROUS. FIVE FEET, TEN INCHES, ONE HUNDRED EIGHTY POUNDS, BLOND HAIR, PALE BLUE EYES. SCARRED UPPER LIP. SHARP AND GANG SUSPECTED OF TAKING TRAIN IN PAIRS AND SINGLY WEEK AGO IN WICHITA POSSIBLE DESTINATION FORT WORTH. CHIEF MURDER TRIAL WITNESS AGAINST SHARP RUMOURED LIVING IN FORT WORTH. NAME CLYDE POPEYE MALLOY. JARIUS WELCH BELIEVED TO BE PART OF GANG. TARRANT COUNTY SHERIFF NOTIFIED.

M. WEBB

'Oh my God!' Cage cried. 'Karalou!'

Johnny grabbed the message and read it.

'Hell, Ben, he's already in Fort Worth,' he said as Cage was starting for the door.

'I know,' Cage shouted back at him. 'And Welch knows about Karalou.'

Cage trotted toward the depot and Johnny followed him, his stomach turning over.

As Cage and Johnny returned to the office after sending the telegram to Fort Worth three men rode up and stopped in front of the office. They dismounted and the older one, a red-faced man with a pot belly walked up to them on the board-walk.

'I'm looking for a Benjamin Cage. Do you know where I can find him?' he said.

'You just found him,' Cage said impatiently. 'I'm Cage. Who are you?'

'I'm Clyde Turnbull, the sheriff of Morgan County,' the man said pulling aside his jacket to reveal his badge. 'And if you're Ben Cage, you're under arrest.'

'Under arrest! What the hell for?' Cage demanded.

'For the murder of a Mr William Benteen,' the sheriff said.

'Who said it was murder?' Cage growled.

'Never you mind about that,' the sheriff said. 'I'll take that pistol you're wearing, Cage.'

'Wait a minute!' Cage yelled. 'What the hell is this?'

One of the sheriff's deputies pointed his pistol at Cage and cocked the hammer.

'Do what he says,' the deputy growled. 'Get your hands up.'

The other deputy had walked around behind Johnny. He put the muzzle of his six-shooter against the back of Johnny's head and grabbed his pistol from its holster.

'Get the manacles on this one,' the sheriff said, nodding his head at Cage.

The first deputy grabbed Cage's arms, pulled them behind him and manacled them together. Immediately, the sheriff grabbed Cage's marshal's badge and ripped it off his shirt. He glanced at it and tossed it into the street.

'This your horse, Cage?' the sheriff asked.

'Yes,' Cage answered from between clenched teeth.

'Get him up on it,' the sheriff ordered.

The first deputy assisted Cage into his saddle.

'Turnbull!' someone yelled. 'What is going on here?'

It was Dick Cartwright. He was hurrying across the street toward the marshal's office.

'Well, Mr Cartwright,' the sheriff said patronizingly, smiling and showing uneven and stained teeth. 'What's going on here is that I have just arrested a cold-blooded killer and I'm taking him to the county lock-up to await trial.'

'They said I murdered Billy Benteen, Mr

Cartwright,' Cage said.

'That's preposterous!' Cartwright cried. 'Who's behind this, your boss at the salt mine?'

'You'd do well to keep your mouth shut,' Turnbull said, the smile melting from his face.

Cartwright was growing livid.

'You can't take him,' he said. 'He's the town marshal. The city council appointed him.'

'Looks to me like your city council is gettin' too damned big for its britches,' Turnbull snarled. 'Who told you that you could do something like that without permission?'

'Times have changed, Turnbull,' Cartwright said, his voice trembling. 'We're not taking any more shit off you and that Colosimo bunch.'

The sheriff looked startled but said nothing in reply. He and his deputies mounted their horses. A deputy took the reins to Cage's horse.

'Watch your mouth, Cartwright,' the sheriff said. 'Somebody might hear you that ain't as charitable as I am.'

'Oh, they're going to hear all right,' the mayor said.

At those words, the bizarre group rode away.

As they rode out of town, Sophie came running up.

'What has happened, Johnny?' she cried. 'Why is Ben going with those men?'

Cartwright stood in the street, thunderstruck. He turned and looked at Johnny.

'They can't do that,' he said.

'It appears they can,' Johnny replied, 'but that ain't the worst of it.'

'What do you mean?' Smith asked. 'How can it get any worse?'

Johnny picked up his six-shooter out of the dirt where the deputy had dropped it.

'Sophie, Mr Cartwright,' he said, 'I have to tell you about Jarius Welch, a girl named Nancy, and John Sharp.'

At the county lock-up in Latona, the county seat, Sheriff Clyde Turnbull ushered Cage into a cell and slammed the door.

'Get used to your accommodations, Cage,' he said. 'You're going to be living here a while.'

Cage surveyed the cell. There was a barred opening in the outside wall. There were no shutters for it and Cage reasoned that if he were still here when winter came, he would have to stuff something in the opening to keep from freezing. There was a bunk attached to the wall at the head and foot with chains attached to anchors in the wall. The chains allowed the bunk to swing up against the wall and latch out of the way when the cell was mopped. The mattress was dirty canvas ticking stuffed unevenly with straw. There was a bucket beneath the bunk for use as a chamberpot.

Turnbull chuckled and started to the door to his office.

'Sheriff,' Cage called. 'Who swore out the complaint against me?'

'Why, it was Billy Benteen's best friend, Luther Scruggs, if it makes any difference.'

'Why am I not surprised?' Cage said. 'Tell me, Sheriff, we've been looking for Mr Scruggs. Did he have any wounds on him?'

'Why do you ask?' Turnbull replied.

'Because a man with a rifle got shot out of the Methodist church belfry yesterday when I was facing Billy Benteen. That person was supposed to shoot me but he didn't get the chance.'

'Now that you mention it,' Turnbull answered with a chuckle, 'he did have a place on his right cheek that looked kind of strange. Looked like it was seeping a little.'

Turnbull went through the door and closed it.

Cage sat down on his bunk and stared at the door.

'I wonder what they are doing back in Blackstone right now?' he asked aloud to no one in particular.

Cage would have been surprised to see what was happening in Blackstone at that moment. Johnny Chance, Brazos Bob Dugan and Raft Townsend walked into the office at Colosimo Mining, just outside Blackstone, pushed past the clerks in the outer office and unceremoniously kicked open the door to the manager's office. Abe Clinton looked up in surprise and started to demand what the intruders wanted when Johnny Chance put a six-shooter to his temple.

'Let's go!' he said.

Luther Scruggs was riding west with copies of three telegraph messages in his pocket. His cousin Earl, the telegrapher, had told him that this was the last time he could do anything for him. Luther smiled to himself at Earl's anguish. He knew that Earl couldn't risk having his jail record exposed to the railway company, but he dismissed his cousin from his mind. His task now was to find five men riding east out of Fort Worth, five men following a leader with a scarred upper lip.

CHAPTER 11

Latona wasn't the late-night town that Blackstone was. By ten o'clock at night most honest town folk were at home and in bed. Latona's one saloon, the Cactus Flower, was still open but rarely more than a dozen locals patronized the establishment late at night.

The streets were almost deserted. For that reason, there were few people around to make note of a wagon approach from the south and pull up the main street. There were two men on the seat of the wagon, and another sitting closely behind them in the wagon bed. Another man, of enormous size, rode alongside on a horse that stood seventeen or eighteen hands high.

Two sheriff's deputies were in the gaol's office. Since they had a prisoner, one planned to spend the night. The other had finished his last patrol and his shift and was about to leave for home and bed. They were idly chatting when they heard the wagon pull up out front. They stopped their talk, listened and exchanged puzzled glances. They got out of their chairs and started to open the front door when it burst open and Raft Townsend stormed into the room. He pointed a twelve-gauge shotgun at their faces.

'Don't make a sound or reach for your gun or I'll blow your teeth all the way to Waxahachie,'* he commanded.

The two wide-eyed deputies threw up their hands and Johnny Chance walked in and disarmed both.

'What you want?' a deputy said.

'Ben Cage and a chat with the sheriff,' Johnny said. 'Where's the sheriff?'

'He's at home,' the senior deputy said.

'You are going to go get him,' Johnny said. 'This big fellow is going to go with you. If anything goes wrong, you die.'

With apprehension, the deputy looked at the hulking Townsend who grinned diabolically and asked, 'How far is it?'

'Not far, 'bout a quarter mile,' the deputy answered in a quavering voice.

'We'll walk,' Townsend said, gesturing to the door with the shotgun. 'Let's go.'

As they walked out, Brazos Bob Dugan and Abe Clinton walked in. Dugan was holding his six-shooter against the back of Abe Clinton's head.

'Mr Clinton?' the deputy asked.

* Town south of Dallas, pronounced Wauks-a-HAT-chee.

'Shut up,' Townsend commanded, poking the deputy in the back with the shotgun.

'Sit down,' Dugan ordered and Clinton sat down.

'Hell, if you want Cage,' said the other deputy, plaintively, 'why don't you just take him and go?'

'Can't do that. We need to have a little heart-to-heart with the sheriff,' Johnny said.

'But we can just . . .' the deputy started.

'Shut the hell up!' Johnny ordered.

The group sat in silence until they heard footsteps on the boardwalk outside. Johnny opened the door.

The sheriff walked in first, followed by the senior deputy. Townsend followed with the shotgun. The sheriff's hair was in disarray and he wore a jacket over his undershirt. He was wearing house slippers.

'Mr Clinton?' he said in disbelief. 'What's happening?'

'We are about to be lynched, you stupid bastard!' Clinton growled. 'Why did you arrest Benjamin Cage?'

Turnbull's mouth fell open.

'Why, he killed Billy. He killed Billy Benteen right in the middle of town. Shot him down in the street.'

'So what, you stupid red-neck bastard?' Clinton spat. 'I've had a .45 pointed at my head for the last five hours thinking each moment was my last.'

'But Benteen was your man,' Turnbull pleaded. 'I brought in his killer.'

Townsend shoved Turnbull into a chair facing Clinton.

Johnny returned his pistol to its holster and stood behind Clinton.

'Talk before somebody gets strung up,' he said.

Clinton glared at Turnbull.

'Did I tell you to arrest Cage?' he asked.

Turnbull stuttered, then said; 'No, I just . . .'

Clinton exploded.

'No, you just what, Turnbull? That kill-crazy son of a bitch outlived his usefulness a long time ago. When Cage shot him down, it was good riddance. He was getting delusions of grandeur. We thought he'd be content with having Blackstone to play with but he was wanting more. It would have been just a question of time before he shot you in the back and took your job, then he would have come after me. It's better for us, and these people here, that he's dead. Do you understand me?'

'Yes, yes, I, uh, yes,' Turnbull stuttered.

'All right, get Cage out of this damned gaol and let him get back to Blackstone. He's got a problem to deal with.'

The sheriff personally unlocked Cage's cell door.

Townsend found Cage's horse and saddle in the gaol barn and brought them around. Townsend and Cage mounted up and Johnny and Dugan climbed onto the wagon. They pulled away and headed south.

Turnbull, his deputies and Clinton stood on the

127

boardwalk and watched them disappear at the end of the street.

'Turnbull,' Clinton asked, 'You got a drink of whiskey in that office of yours?'

'I was thinking the same thing,' a sagging Turnbull said.

As Cage rode beside Johnny through the night back toward Blackstone, he noticed his friend was quieter than usual. Cage knew that an adventure such as the one they had experienced would have given Johnny the energy to talk endlessly for the whole trip.

'What's wrong?' Cage asked eventually. 'Did you hear back from Fort Worth?'

Without looking at him, Johnny said, 'Yes.'

Panic rose in Cage's throat.

'What was it?' he demanded.

'Ben,' Johnny said hoarsely, 'I have awful bad news. It's about Karalou. The sheriff sent a deputy out to her place to stay with her but Welch had already been there. She's dead.'

Cage reined his horse to a stop and dismounted. Dugan, driving the wagon, shouted: 'Whoa!'

Cage walked off the road and fell to his knees. Johnny dismounted and walked to him.

Dugan and Townsend had known of the message and were dreading the moment when Cage had to be told. They sat silently, watching.

'My God, what have I done?' Cage asked the night.

Johnny was puzzled.

'What do you mean, pal? You haven't done anything.'

'Yes, I have,' Cage answered. 'I didn't kill Welch when I had the chance. I sat down with Nancy and marked her for death. Karalou loved me and now she's dead.'

Cage woke at dawn the next morning. He looked around the room but recognized nothing. His head hurt above his eyes and there was a horrible taste in his mouth. He remembered drinking the whiskey and being terribly sleepy, but that had been at Lee and Sophie's house.

He sat up on the side of the bed and was surprised that he was still wearing his jeans. At that moment the bedroom door opened and Sophie walked in, carrying a mug. She was wearing a dressing-gown.

'I thought you would be waking right about now,' she said. 'Here's some coffee.'

'Is this your bed?' he asked.

'Yes it is,' she replied. 'At least I persuaded you to take off your boots before you got in it last night.'

'Where did you sleep?'

'Right here beside you.'

'My God! We didn't—'

'No, we most certainly did not,' she interrupted. 'I stayed because you needed someone with you. I have never seen whiskey work so fast on anyone before. Now I know why you don't drink whiskey.'

'I'm sorry if I was a nuisance,' he said, sipping the coffee.

'You were not a nuisance,' she replied. 'You were suffering from grief, a guilty conscience and God knows what else, but you weren't a nuisance.'

'What did I say?' he asked sheepishly.

'You talked about Nancy and how young and innocent she was and what happened to her and that it was your fault. You talked about Karalou and you said that her death was your fault. You were feeling awfully guilty about those girls but nothing I said seemed to change your mind.'

She fell silent, watching him drink the coffee. He was content to let the strong brew clear the cobwebs and dampen his headache.

'Is there going to be more violence?' she asked softly.

'If those men come here, I'm afraid there is no way to avoid it, much as I'd like to,' he replied. 'I'd rather capture them and see them tried for what they've done. Shooting them is too fast, too merciful. I want to see Welch pay for what he's done.'

'Some time,' she said gently, 'can we talk about Karalou?'

'Yes,' he said. 'Sometime. When I'm up to it.'

'Did you love her?'

'I cared for her very much.'

'We can leave it at that for right now,' she said. 'Get dressed. I'm making breakfast. You have a meeting with the city fathers this morning.'

When Cage walked into the kitchen, Johnny was drinking coffee and talking to Lee.

'Ben, I forgot to tell you last night,' Johnny said. 'They found Popeye Malloy floating in the Trinity River yesterday. They identified him from his belt buckle. From what the sheriff's telegraph message said, they worked him over before they killed him.'

'So the Sharp-Welch gang has finished its chores in Fort Worth,' Cage said,

'That would seem to be,' Johnny agreed. 'But what will they do now? Would Welch come all this way to kill Karalou or might he have something else in mind?'

'John,' Cage said, 'we have no way of knowing but we are going to plan as if he was coming here with the whole gang.'

Sophie put plates of scrambled eggs and bacon in front of the three of them. Then she put a plate stacked with biscuits in the middle of the table along with a bowl of butter and a jar of peach preserves.

'That's the best I can do right now, fellows, I have to dress for work,' Sophie said.

Later that morning, Cage and Johnny sat down with Dick Cartwright and the other city councilmen.

Cage was encouraged to see that they all looked concerned but determined.

'I have three men deputized as deputy marshals,' said Cage. 'That's Chance, Dugan and Townsend.

We can use some more help from the townspeople.'

Dick Cartwright stood up.

'I can think of half a dozen men here in town who have experience either in the war or fighting Indians,' he said. 'They know what it is to be under fire. I'll talk to each of them to make certain they are armed and available to help out.'

'Make darn sure they know what they are doing, Mr Cartwright,' Cage said. 'I don't want any of my deputies to get shot in the back while they are fighting Sharp's people.'

'I want my people armed with carbines,' Cage continued. 'They are easier to handle in this kind of fight. We have only one. Where can I get two more?'

'Ansley over at the gun store can supply 'em,' Cartwright answered. 'He's one of those I was telling you about. He said for whatever you need just let him know.'

'Johnny,' Cage said, 'After we are through here, you see Ansley about the carbines and ammunition.'

Johnny nodded.

'All right folks,' Cage continued, 'we don't know when they are going to be here, but we can set up to give them a greeting no matter when they show up.'

Cage gave them their assignments. John Chance would be stationed in the land office across the street from the bank. Johnny would keep an eye on the bank through the land office's window.

Townsend would be next door to the bank in the saddler's shop. Dugan would be inside the bank, dressed as a clerk and seated at a desk. Cage would roam the street in the vicinity of the bank. The townsmen who were asked to use a firearm would have their weapons ready for action when they heard the first shot. They were to take action if Cage and his deputies failed to stop the bank robbers.

'Let's hope this is all for nothing,' Cage told them, 'and that that gang doesn't show up here. But wishing won't slice bacon, so we are going to be ready.'

When the meeting ended, Cage's deputies hurried over to Ansley's gun store to get their carbines and the other volunteers dispersed to their offices or places of business. Cage walked down to the general store and talked to Lee while Sophie was with a customer.

'Lee,' he said, 'I want you to stay here with Sophie. I don't know how much Welch knows about our business here, but if he knows about Sophie, he will try to do something to her. Are you armed?'

Lee pulled a sawed-off shotgun from beneath the counter.

'I'm not a sure-shot like yourself, Ben,' he said. 'I need something where I just point it in the general direction.'

'That should do the trick,' Cage said.

'I keep this hidden from Sophie. She doesn't like firearms of any kind,' Lee added.

'That's what I've found out,' Cage said. 'She said she was afraid of me after Oleman and I shot it out.'

'That was the damndest thing I ever saw, Ben,' Lee whispered. 'She loved you but she couldn't reconcile her feelings with what you did to Oleman. She was so confused, she didn't know what she was doing.'

'When she was standing over Benteen's body, she wasn't confused,' Cage said.

Lee nodded.

'Revenge has a lot of weight, Ben,' he said.

Morning passed and noon arrived. Cage had Grace Hollis send lunches to the boys at their stations so they could eat and keep watch. Word had gotten around town, so the number of people on the street had dwindled to a few. As Cage strolled the board-walk he could see faces at the windows of businesses and offices, peering down the street toward the bank.

Three o'clock came and went. Cage stared at each person coming down the street, searching their faces for some tell-tale sign of evil intent. From a block away, he watched riders, wagon drivers and walkers enter the bank, then walk out again, taking care of their personal business.

Cage went into Grace Hollis's café and got a mug of coffee. He stood out front on the boardwalk to sip it.

Four horsemen rode by going in the direction of

the bank. Cage stiffened as they went by and he watched them ride on by the bank. In a few minutes, two more horsemen rode by and Cage scrutinized them closely. Grace walked out of the café door and looked at the riders.

'I know those boys,' she said. 'They work on the Helms spread over by Kirburg.'

The tension left Cage's body.

'Thanks, Grace,' he said. 'I thought they looked like bad men.'

'They may be bad but they ain't no bank-robbers,' Grace cackled.

Cage finished his coffee and handed the mug to Grace.

'I think I'll mosey on down the street, Grace,' he said.

'Good luck.'

Cage glanced at the bank. A pair of horsemen had ridden up from the south end of town and were strolling to the bank's door.

Cage crossed the street and walked south. He was about a block from the bank and on the opposite side of the street when he met Dick Cartwright.

Cartwright dabbed at his forehead with a hand-kerchief.

'I must be on edge, Ben,' he said. 'As I was walk-ing up here, I saw a man with a scarred upper lip and for a moment, I thought he was John Sharp. But he smiled and tipped his hat and said, "Afternoon, Mayor". So must be from around here.'

'Had you ever seen him before?' Cage asked, watching as another horseman rode up to the bank and dismounted.

'As a matter of fact, no,' Cartwright said, glancing back down the boardwalk.

'I'll think I'll go check into it,' Cage said. 'What was he wearing?'

Cartwright thought for a moment.

'Black hat, tan shirt and jeans, I believe.'

As Cage started up the street, another rider stopped at the bank and dismounted. Cage glanced at him, then back to the man whose looks had unsettled Cartwright. He was leaning against a post on Cage's side of the street opposite the bank. At that moment, there was a shot from within the bank. Townsend came out of the saddler's shop and the man in the black hat drew his pistol and aimed at Townsend.

The land-office door burst open and Matthews, the land agent, came out, levering a round into the breech of his rifle. He didn't see the man standing not ten feet to his right with his pistol in his hand. Cage shouted a warning but it came too late. The black-hatted man shot Matthews down, then turned and again took aim at Townsend.

The ambushers were being ambushed!

CHAPTER 12

Townsend heard Cage's shouts and turned in time to see a man in a black hat drawing a bead on him. He snapped off a shot from the waist and fell to the ground. Cage drew his .45 as he ran. One of the men who had gone into the bank emerged, blue bandanna over his face and pistol held in front. He glanced quickly about, saw Cage running and Sharp providing cover, turned and shouted something into the bank's door. Two more of the men backed out of the bank door, pistols leveled and carrying canvas bags in their left hands. One wore a red bandanna over his lower face and a gray hat. The other wore a greasy white kerchief and a brown hat. A shot rang out from the bank and the fourth robber staggered backward through the door, dropping his bag of loot. Red bandanna picked up the bag and helped the wounded man to his feet. All four started to mount their horses. Townsend squirmed into a prone firing position and shot blue bandanna as he was swinging his right leg over his horse. The man fell off the horse's left side into the dirt and lay still. Sharp fired again at Townsend. Cage fired a quick shot at Sharp to spoil his aim at Townsend. The shot missed Sharp but smashed a window behind him, catching his attention. He turned a wolfish glare at Cage and fired. Cage heard the shot buzz past his ear and dived forward to the ground, firing another shot as he fell.

Johnny fired from the title office and the wounded robber pitched forward onto his mount's neck. As the horse moved forward, the dead man rolled backward off the horse over its tail. The remaining two spurred their mounts to a gallop directly toward Cage, one behind the other. Johnny fired another shot that broke brown hat's shoulder and made him drop his moneybag into the street. Red bandanna spurred his mount toward Cage, intent on riding him down. Cage couldn't get a clear shot at the rider so fired at the easiest target, the horse. The horse's front legs buckled and the animal pitched headlong into the dirt. When the rider felt the horse start to go down he got his feet out of the stirrups. Cage rolled to his left out of the dying animal's path, dimly aware that another one of Sharp's bullets kicked up the dirt by his face. The fallen rider rolled and came to rest on his back in a cloud of dust. He had lost his six-shooter in the fall but as he struggled to his feet, he pulled another from his boot. Turning, he spotted Cage through the dust a few paces away and raised his weapon for what appeared to be an easy shot. Cage fired first. The robber pitched backward and his shot went into the air.

Cage turned to fire at Sharp but he had disappeared. Dugan ran out of the bank.

Johnny ran out of the land office and mounted one of the two horses in front of the bank.

'The other one is wounded and went down the alley,' he yelled.

'Go after him!' Cage shouted.

Johnny spurred the horse to a gallop and disappeared down the alley where the wounded robber had fled.

Grimsby the undertaker drove up in his wagon and was stunned by the scene. He stepped down and bent over red bandanna. Suddenly, he gasped and jumped back.

'He's alive!' he shouted.

Cage strode to where the man lay in a widening pool of blood, struggling for breath, his eyes wide and staring. Cage pulled the bandanna from the man's face to see a trickle of blood running from the corner of his mouth.

Cage leaned over the dying man and said: 'Was Sharp your lookout?'

For a few moments it appeared that the man did not understand, then his eyes focused on Cage's face and he grinned bizarrely, blood staining his teeth.

'He figured you'd be waiting,' the outlaw gurgled.

'That's what I thought,' Cage said to Dugan. 'He was the advance scout himself. Clever bastard.'

'You're Cage, ain't ye?' the man whispered. 'They goin' cook that sweet meat of yourn right off the bone.'

'What?' Cage said. 'What do you mean?'

The bandit struggled to get the words out, saying: 'They goin' to fix you . . .' That was as far as he got before his words ended in a gurgle and his eyes lost focus.

'What in hell was all that?' Townsend asked.

'I don't know,' Cage answered. 'But I don't like the sound of it.'

'What happened in the bank?' Cage asked.

'Two of 'em came in and pulled their pistols and asked for all the cash,' said Dugan. 'Then the other two came in right behind them. The one that held his gun on me was mean-looking. I could see the hatred in his eyes while I filled his bag. I'm supposing he didn't like my looks because when he was backing out the door, he stopped and drew a bead on me. By then I had my .44 in my hand and I fired first. Surprised the hell out of 'im.'

Suddenly a man ran up and shouted: 'There's someone hurt up at the general store!'

Cage's blood seemed to freeze in his veins and he started to run toward the store.

A crowd of the curious was grouped around the

front door of the store. Cage forced his way into the interior. Lee lay in the middle of the floor, blood from a body wound spreading beneath him. Cage ran into the back room. The back door had been penetrated by two gunshots and was standing open. Sophie was nowhere in sight. There were wagon tracks in the alley.

Cage returned to Lee's side.

'What happened, Lee?' he cried.

'Someone knocked on the back door and called me by name, wanting to come in. When I started to unlock the door, they fired through the door. I ran in here and fell. It was Luther. Luther and another man.' He paused, biting his lip and sobbed: 'They took Sophie, Ben, they took her.'

'Someone get the doctor for Lee,' Cage ordered and rushed out the door and down the street to his office. He got his horse and galloped back to the bank.

Cage rode up and yelled at Dugan and Townsend: 'They shot Lee Garrett and they've got Sophie!'

'Oh God, no!' Dugan exclaimed. He ran to the remaining horse tied in front of the bank. Townsend ran back to the gaol for his.

Cage was about to say: Let's trail Johnny, when Johnny himself rode into view two blocks away down the main street. He held the reins of a horse with a dead man draped across the saddle.

Cage, Townsend and Dugan rode up alongside and stopped.

'Where was he going?' Cage asked.

'Heading out to the north,' Johnny said. 'He was easy to track, left a trail of blood all the way out the north of town.'

Cage said: 'They've taken Sophie.'

'Oh hell's fire!' Johnny exclaimed.

'They must have had a rendezvous point somewhere to the north.' Cage said.

'That's a safe bet,' Johnny said, handing the reins of the dead man's horse to a startled bystander. 'What's to the north of town,' he asked the man.

The man hesitated, then said: 'Why, the cotton gin, I suppose and, er, I suppose there's the slaughterhouse too.'

Cage thought his heart had stopped in his chest.

'The slaughterhouse,' he yelled. 'That bastard said they were going to cook the sweetmeat . . .'

Cage spurred his mount into a gallop. Dugan and Townsend followed. Dugan explained to Johnny about what the bank robber had said just before he died.

The quartet rode until they met a county road crew knocking off from work.

Reining to a stop, Cage shouted: 'Have you men seen a wagon go by here with two men on it, probably in a hurry?'

'Sure have, Sheriff,' the foreman replied. One feller was driving and t'other one was in the back holding down some critter under a tarp.'

'Thank you,' Cage cried and they spurred their

horses to another gallop.

They could smell the slaughterhouse about the time they could see it. It stood to the west of the northbound road, about a mile beyond the cotton gin. As they approached, they could see an unattended flatbed wagon in front and three saddled horses hitched to a rail by a watering-trough.

'Dugan, Townsend, you two go around either side and come in from the back. Johnny and I will go in the front,' Cage instructed.

The slaughterhouse had shut down for the day. The few pigs in the pens in back would live to see another dawn. The steam engine that supplied the pulley-power for the conveyors was silent. When Cage entered the front door, he saw two bodies. One appeared to be a clerk and the other looked to be the stoker who kept the coal fires burning beneath the scalding tank and the rendering vat so that they were ready for the next day's slaughter. The two tanks contained too much liquid for the crew to allow them to grow cold. The unfortunate little man assigned to stoke the fires overnight had done his job for the last time. The scalding tank was ready for the hogs after their throats were cut and their blood collected. The conveyer would lower them a half-dozen at a time into the boiling water in preparation for skinning and butchering.

With his heart in his throat, Cage peered around the corner of the door into the work area. He heard a voice saying:

'Get on with it, Welch. Those damned law men are goin' to figure it all out any minute.'

It was the wolf-faced man with the ugly lip speaking. Sharp stood on the work floor by the rendering vat looking upward. He was holding a rope in his hands. Cage eased further into the room and to his horror saw that the rope extended to a pulley on an overhead beam. The other end of the rope went to a catwalk where Welch was tying the rope to Sophie's wrists. Her hands and legs were bound and most of her clothes were torn off. Her eyes were blank as if she was stunned. The Gibson Girl blouse was gone and her undergarments were shredded.

The rendering vat was directly beneath her!

CHAPTER 13

Cage was too far away to risk a pistol shot at Welch. He could shoot Sharp but Welch would still be able to throw Sophie over the rail of the catwalk into the vat. He backed up and cast about frantically for a stair or ladder.

He saw a stairway in a dark recess.

He turned to Johnny and whispered, 'I'm going up there. Wait until I get their attention, then get that rope away from Sharp.'

The stairs took him to a landing that circled the perimeter of the slaughterhouse's main work area. A catwalk extended across the entire work area providing maintenance access to the conveyor system that transported the animal carcasses from one workstation to another.

Welch was still trying to tie the rope around Sophie's wrists but she was struggling.

'Damn it, Luther!' Sharp called out. 'Get your ass out there and give him a hand so we can get out of here.'

Cage leaned around the corner far enough to see Welch and Sophie. Welch was fumbling with the rope and trying to hold Sophie still. Another man walked out onto the catwalk toward them. It was Luther!

Cage took the four-shot Cloverleaf out of his boot and put it in his right-hand jacket pocket.

Sharp again shouted at Welch to get on with it.

'I want her naked when we lower her in,' Welch answered back.

'I'll hold her. You tie,' said Luther. He leered at the half-naked girl and said: 'I'm goin' to hold you real good.'

Cage walked out onto the landing and up to the catwalk. Welch saw him immediately and sudden fear contorted his face.

'It's Cage! Shoot the son of a bitch!' he screamed.

Luther looked at Cage and paled. Sharp looked up in surprise. Sharp started to draw.

'Leave it!' Johnny shouted and Sharp froze.

Townsend and Dugan moved into the work area behind Sharp.

Luther pulled his pistol from its holster. Cage took one step to his right so he wouldn't endanger Sophie and fired. The shot hit Luther in the upper chest. He staggered backward, dropping his pistol. Turning, he tried to run but his legs collapsed and he fell on the catwalk.

Welch yelled to Cage: 'Drop the gun or I'll kill her.' He pulled Sophie to her feet and shielded himself with her body, holding his pistol to her head. He was inching his way backward along the catwalk.

'You can't get out of here alive, Welch,' Cage said. 'Give it up.'

'Drop the gun, Cage!' Welch shouted. 'I don't give a damn if you get me but I'll have the satisfaction of killing your bitch in front of your eyes before I die. Drop it!'

Cage hesitated a moment, then carefully placed the .44 on the floor.

Welch gloated evilly and leveled his pistol at Cage.

'Now Mr high and mighty, it's my turn,' he yelled.

When Welch extended his arm away from Sophie's head to aim at Cage, it was the opening that Dugan had been waiting for. He fired and the pistol flew from Welch's hand. Welch screamed in pain as the shot smashed two fingers on his right hand. In desperation Welch grabbed Sophie and lifted her over the catwalk railing.

Screaming, 'No, no you bastard!' Cage rushed frantically at Welch, drawing the little Colt from his jacket pocket. Sophie was screaming as she squirmed and twisted to keep Welch off balance. In a split second, Cage was upon them, reaching for the girl, but Welch, with a superhuman effort born of hatred and madness, pushed her over the railing. As she went over and started to fall, her eyes were on Cage, wide and pleading.

'Drop her in, Sharp!' Welch screamed.

With a scream of primal fury, Cage leaped at Welch and they crashed down on the catwalk. Cage fired blindly with the small pistol and Welch cried out when the bullet tore through the flesh on his right side. Welch's arm lashed out and knocked the pistol from Cage's hand and it fell to the work floor below.

Sharp looked up and hesitated for a split second as Sophie swung out over the vat. Then he grinned and let go of the rope. Townsend ran at Sharp, butting him with his shoulder and grabbing for the rope. Sophie's weight pulled three feet of the rope through Townsend's hand, burning it and bringing blood. Ignoring the pain, he tightened his grip until he could get his other hand on the rope. He stopped it with Sophie's feet clearing the scalding fat by not more than a hand's length.

Sharp started to get up but Johnny put his six-shooter in the bank robber's face. 'Give me a reason!' he said.

Sophie was swinging like a pendulum, her feet sweeping less than a foot from the boiling grease. Dugan ran to the vat and leaned out dangerously over the cauldron. As Sophie swung sickeningly toward them, he grabbed her legs and pulled her away from danger.

'We've got her, Cage,' yelled Townsend.

Welch got to his feet, turned and started to run toward the far end of the catwalk, but Cage caught him by the collar from behind and dragged him to a stop. As Welch spun to face Cage, he drew a knife. His motion carried him into Luther, rolling the wounded man off the catwalk. There was a cry, then a splash as Luther fell into the scalding tank. A split second later, Luther clawed his way to the surface of the boiling water and shrieked with the agony of a lost soul, his hands reaching skyward as if for mercy. The men on the floor looked up in horror at the agonized, despairing cry. Quickly the scream trailed away as the bubbly, greasy brown water mercifully closed over Luther's head.

Welch slashed at Cage's face with a hunting-knife in his left hand. Cage released him and jumped back, throwing up his right arm. He felt the knife catch his sleeve and lay it open. Welch slashed again in a backhand motion to his left then back again but Cage was ready. Cage leaned back to dodge the blade, then stepped in with a roundhouse right to Welch's face. The momentum of Welch's left-handed slash overbalanced him to his right and the impact of Cage's fist knocked him against the low railing and he flipped over it. Welch saw the hot grease beneath him.

Welch grabbed frantically at the bottom rail with his left hand and caught it with his fingertips his eyes wide in panic. His grip was slipping and a shrill sound came from his throat.

Cage grabbed his wrist stopping the slide. He got his other hand beneath Welch's shoulder and pulled him back onto the catwalk. The searing pain in Welch's side sapped what strength he had left and he sprawled on his face.

Welch turned his head to the side so that he could see Cage with one eye.

'Why?' he asked between gasps. 'Why did you pull me back up?'

'So justice can be served,' Cage answered.

Welch grimaced and laughed his strange sobbing laugh.

'Mr straight-shooter Ben Cage. I was goin' to cook that pretty meat right off that quim of yours and you saved my ass,' he said. 'Good God, nobody's that damned holy!'

Cage looked at the laughing face before him and glanced down at the rendering-vat. He knew he could get away with it. He could say that Welch was struggling to get away and lost his balance. He thought about Nancy's smiling face and Karalou in his arms. He lifted Welch to his feet and bent him over the railing so he could see the hot oil below.

Welch gasped, then whimpered like a schoolgirl.

Cage half-pushed, half-carried Welch off the catwalk and down the steps to the work floor.

Sophie was sitting on a bench with Dugan's coat around her, staring blankly at the floor.

Cage found some cloth and made a makeshift bandage for the wound in Welch's side. It appeared that the bullet had torn through his flesh but had struck no vital organ. Cage dragged Welch to the post where Townsend had manacled Sharp and manacled him to it with his hands behind him. Only then did he go to Sophie's side.

He knelt before her so he could look into her face. Her eyes went out of focus when she looked at Cage and her face was expressionless. She stared at him blankly for what seemed to him a long time, then there was a flicker of recognition.

'Sophie,' Cage said, taking her hands in his. 'Are you all right? Did he hurt you?'

She looked at him and spoke slowly, as in a dream.

'No, I'm just bruised a little. I'm not hurt. I'm still alive.'

The vacant, detached tone of her voice bothered Cage and he knew he should get her back to town and to the doctor as quickly as possible.

'I'll be right back,' he said.

Cage walked to where Johnny stood. 'We'll use their wagon. Load Sharp and Welch in the back and tie them down. I'll take Sophie . . .'

Suddenly Sharp screamed hysterically: 'No, don't let her! Don't let her!'

Cage spun around. Johnny looked up and gasped. Dugan, on his way out the door, stopped, spun and froze.

Cage had forgotten the boot pistol he'd dropped during the struggle with Welch on the catwalk. Sophie had found it! She was standing in front of Welch with Cage's Cloverleaf pointed at the two outlaws. Sharp was whimpering and scrambling to hide behind the post; his movements jerked Welch around so he stared directly into the muzzle of the .41 Colt.

Before Cage could move, Sophie said in a rasping voice: 'This is for Nancy.'

She fired into Welch's thigh.

Welch grunted and buckled but was held erect by the manacles on his wrists.

'No, no, please God, no!' he screamed.

Cage ran toward Sophie, ordering her to drop the gun.

Sophie ignored his cries and said: 'This is for Karalou,' and fired directly into Welch's crotch. Blood spurted from Welch's genitals, and unspeakable pain distorted his face. His mouth opened in a silent scream.

Cage was still eight feet away when Sophie said: 'And this is for me,' and fired the third shot.

A dark hole appeared above Welch's right eye and the back of his head erupted. He slumped to the floor, his shattered head leaking blood over his knees.

CHAPTER 14

It was late November in Rio Diablo and a leaden sky in the north-east heralded the approach of a 'blue norther'. Marshal Benjamin Cage was on his way home late in a long and difficult day. He thought to himself that since he was tired, hungry and depressed the dreary weather made a perfect back-drop for his mood. He had attended a town-council meeting and sat through the petty bickering, then had to subdue four unruly cowboys who insisted on shooting up the establishments on the main street for their amusement. After knocking two of them unconscious, he disarmed the remaining pair and got them all comfortably settled in the gaol.

John Sharp had recently vacated one of the gaol cells when two federal marshals came to take him back to Kansas for an overdue date with the hang-man. His gang was dead, including the old crony he'd added to it in Fort Worth. Cage had the plea-sure of seeing the outlaw and his escorts off at the depot and wishing them a pleasant trip.

Cage and Johnny had yet another occasion to mourn for someone close to them. They learned, by communications from Marshal Webb in Dodge City, that Elzee Laroux had indeed 'cold trailed' Sharp and Welch. He had caught up with the gang in Wichita, Kansas but they recognized him. Wichita authorities found him and contacted Webb because of documents found on the body. One of the documents was an unmailed letter addressed to Benjamin Cage in Blackstone, Texas. It had been wadded up and thrown down beside Elzee's body. Welch had known from a few days after his escape where Cage could be found.

Lee Garrett recovered from his wound with difficulty but eventually returned to work at the general store. Dugan dropped the 'Brazos' from his name when he became a full-time deputy marshal. Townsend also decided to stay on with Cage as a deputy.

Johnny Chance preferred something other than law work so he went into partnership with Brewster at the Black Stallion. Johnny added some tables and a roulette wheel to the saloon's attractions and ran that end of the business. Because he ran a straight game, he and Brewster did quite well.

The cause of Cage's depression was the trauma that Sophie suffered from her ordeal. She was recovering slowly from her shock, at times declaring herself fit but at other times suffering periods of uncontrollable weeping. She never mentioned the way that Welch died that day at the slaughterhouse and Cage did not know if she even remembered executing Welch. He decided just to comfort her the best he knew how until the trauma of that day had been dulled by time. He had spoken secretly to old Doc Whiddon about her condition and the horrific circumstances that had brought it on. The doctor said it was a tribute to her strength that she wasn't a raving lunatic after what she had endured. All he could offer was a recommendation to treat her gently and with understanding and let time do its work.

Cage and Sophie had married in a quiet, private ceremony so that Cage could stay close to her in her convalescence. After Lee recovered from his wound and no longer needed Sophie's help around the house, the two of them had moved to their own home, a modest house on the edge of town, his destination this night.

Cage arrived home and got his mount settled down in the stable with a blanket over her back and a full serving of oats. He entered the house quietly and found a cold supper waiting on the kitchen table, covered with a white cloth. After he ate, he tiptoed down the hall to the bedroom he shared with Sophie.

She had refused any romantic overtures since that day at the slaughterhouse and the coldness of their relationship disturbed him deeply. He had suggested separate sleeping arrangements but

Sophie said no; she wanted the reassuring presence of him beside her in the night.

He undressed quietly by the light of the low fire in the fireplace and slipped beneath the covers trying not to wake her.

As he settled down for sleep, there was a stirring on the other side of the bed. Sophie turned on to her side facing him. He could see her face dimly by the light of the low fire so he reached over and touched her cheek gently, savoring the warmth and silky softness of it. He sighed and pulled the covers over his chest and started to settle in for a richly deserved night's sleep. There was another movement in the bed and a warm arm slipped across his chest. Then a warm, naked body pressed against his side and a full, supple thigh slid over his hip.

'Hey cowboy, new in town?' came Sophie's voice in a husky whisper.

'Matter of fact, ma'am, I am,' he answered.

'Where have you been all this time?'

'Out on the range, rustling longhorns.'

'How about rustling something else for a change?'

'Talked me plumb into it, ma'am.'

She was back.